"I will kill you!"

Still half-asleep and completely naked, Dylan rolled over and stared at the enraged Lord Perronet at the door of his bedchamber.

The man's face was as red as a cherry and—most surprising of all—he was fumbling for the sword at his side.

Now wide-awake, Dylan reached for his own weapon, which should have been beside his bed. He halted in stunned shock as his hand encountered an unexpected mound.

That moved.

"Uncle?" Genevieve Perronet said as she sat up, holding the coverings over herself.

It was obvious that beneath those coverings she was as naked as he.

"I'm going to kill you for what you've done!" Lord Perronet roared, finally succeeding in drawing his sword.

Dylan leapt from the bed, searching frantically for his weapon.

What had he done with it last night?

What had he done last night, period!

Dear Reader,

Entertainment. Escape. Fantasy. These three words describe the heart of Harlequin Historical novels. If you want compelling, emotional stories by some of the best writers in the field, look no further.

After recently publishing her first mainstream historical romance for Avon Books, award-winning author Margaret Moore returns this month with a terrific "opposites attract" story, *The Welshman's Bride.* Part of Margaret's ongoing WARRIOR SERIES, this is the tale of a roguish Welsh nobleman who must marry a shy chatelaine after the two are caught in a compromising situation. Don't miss the humor and passion as they learn to appreciate their differences and fall in love!

Hunter of My Heart is a fresh and exciting Regency by talented newcomer Janet Kendall featuring two Scottish nobles who are bribed into marrying to protect their past secrets. And be sure to look for Laurie Grant's final DEVLIN BROTHERS book, *Maggie and the Maverick,* about two wounded souls who share friendship and love under Texas skies.

Rounding out the month is *The Unlikely Wife* by Cassandra Austin, an author known for her stories of emotion and drama. Here, the flirty Rebecca Huntington is *truly* an unlikely wife—until officer and gentleman Clark Forrester shows her what the love of a good man can do!

Whatever your tastes in reading, you'll be sure to find a romantic journey back to the past between the covers of a Harlequin Historical® novel.

Sincerely,

Tracy Farrell
Senior Editor

Please address questions and book requests to:
Harlequin Reader Service
U.S.: 3010 Walden Ave., P.O. Box 1325, Buffalo, NY 14269
Canadian: P.O. Box 609, Fort Erie, Ont. L2A 5X3

THE WELSHMAN'S BRIDE

Margaret Moore

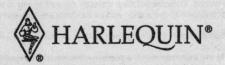

HARLEQUIN®

TORONTO • NEW YORK • LONDON
AMSTERDAM • PARIS • SYDNEY • HAMBURG
STOCKHOLM • ATHENS • TOKYO • MILAN • MADRID
PRAGUE • WARSAW • BUDAPEST • AUCKLAND

ISBN 0-373-29059-4

THE WELSHMAN'S BRIDE

Books by Margaret Moore

MARGARET MOORE

Award-winning author Margaret Moore began her career at the age of eight, when she and a friend concocted stories featuring a lovely damsel and a handsome, misunderstood thief nicknamed "The Red Sheik."

Unknowingly pursuing her destiny, Margaret graduated with distinction from the University of Toronto with a Bachelor of Arts degree. She has been a Leading Wren in the Royal Canadian Naval Reserve, an award-winning public speaker, a member of an archery team, and a student of fencing and ballroom dancing. She has also worked for every major department store chain in Canada.

Margaret sold her first historical romance, A WARRIOR'S HEART, to Harlequin Historicals in 1991. She has recently completed her eighteenth novel for Harlequin. Margaret lives in Toronto with her husband, two children and two cats.

With thanks to "the Fam," for their witty repartée
and help with the housework.

Chapter One

"Don't be daft!" Dylan DeLanyea exclaimed with a roguish grin as he regarded his unsmiling cousin.

His head cradled in his hands, his feet crossed at the ankles, Dylan lay upon the large bed in the chamber made over to his use while he visited his uncle at the castle of Craig Fawr. "Not serious, me, and she knows it. You could have saved yourself some trouble and stayed in the hall with your wife."

"How can you be so sure what she thinks?" Griffydd demanded, his arms folded over his broad, muscular chest. "If I did not know you well, I would think you were wooing Genevieve Perronet with marriage in mind."

Dylan shook his head, his eyes twinkling merrily. "Everybody knows I'm not ready to be married, and I'm too young, besides."

"Not ready, maybe—but you're older than I am," the newly wedded Griffydd reminded him.

"Just because you've got yourself a wife doesn't mean everybody thinks of marriage. I was only enjoying the young lady's company."

"Lady Genevieve Perronet is already betrothed."

"There, then!" Dylan cried triumphantly, shifting to a sitting position. "She can't think I'm serious."

"People have broken their betrothals before this, and I hear you've been doing a little more than talking to her," Griffydd said, looking at Dylan with grim intensity.

Dylan flushed. "A few chaste kisses hardly count as trying to break a betrothal," he replied, wondering if one of the nosy castle servants had seen him with her and gossiped.

"For you, perhaps. It could be Genevieve Perronet thinks differently. She has led a very sheltered life with Lady Katherine."

"And now she's free for a short while. I don't see anything wrong with amusing her."

"Tell that to her intended. Lord Kirkheathe might take a different view."

"Well, as I am an honorable knight, I would never come between a man and his future wife," Dylan said with genuine conviction.

"And you are being honorable, aren't you?"

"God's wounds, what's that supposed to mean?"

"You aren't trying to seduce her?"

"I've considered it."

"Dylan!"

"But only considered," he assured Griffydd jovially. "She's a well-bred, betrothed lady for whom I have the greatest respect, for one thing. And for another, there's her uncle. Norman to the bones, that one, all gloom and ambition. I wouldn't want to get on the wrong side of him."

"I'm glad you've realized that. Her uncle does not strike me as a forgiving man, should his plans for her be thwarted."

"They won't be, although I must say it is a waste to marry one so young to one so old. Kirkheathe must be—what? Sixty?"

"Forty."

Dylan stretched, his movements lithe as a panther. "Making too much of this you are, Griffydd."

"Making too little of her feelings you are,"

Griffydd retorted. "A woman's heart is not something to be toyed with."

"We're both enjoying the game, that's all," Dylan insisted. "And if she's a little sad when she leaves here, I see nothing so wrong in that. I will be sad to see her go, too."

"So you like her, then?"

"Of course. What is there not to be liked? She's young, she's pretty, she laughs when I make a joke." Dylan leaned conspiratorially closer. "She's as shapely a woman as ever I've seen, and her kisses—chaste though they were—were very pleasant."

"You are beyond redemption," Griffydd growled.

"Nonsense! I've done nothing that requires redemption."

"Did you tell her about your children?"

Dylan frowned. "There was no occasion to mention them. We are having a little harmless fun before she marries that ancient knight, is all."

"You are absolutely certain she understands that is how you feel?"

Dylan could not quite meet Griffydd's steadfast gaze. "I said so, didn't I? I've given her no reason to think otherwise."

"I hope you're right. I wouldn't want anything

to spoil these celebrations. This is Trystan's time. He's worked hard for his knighthood, and I don't want the festivities disrupted because you can't keep it in your breeches."

Dylan scowled. "*Anwyl*, listen to you! I told you, I haven't done any harm. And speaking of Trystan, should you not be seeing if your little brother has recovered from his vigil and his knighting? It's long past noon, and he was still asleep the last time I looked. I hope he'll be well enough to attend tonight's feast."

Griffydd nodded as he rose from the stool. "You will be at the feast?"

"Where else?"

Griffydd raised an eyebrow.

"Maybe I do have a notion to go see Bertha at the village tavern, for old times' sake."

Griffydd shook his head. "You're hopeless," he muttered as he strode through the door.

"Only joking, me!" Dylan called out as the door banged.

For a moment, an uncharacteristically serious expression appeared on his darkly handsome face, then, being Dylan, the expression disappeared, replaced by a merry grin.

He rose from the bed and started to whistle as

he went to see if pretty Lady Genevieve would keep their rendezvous in his aunt's garden.

Genevieve pulled her fur-lined cloak more tightly around herself as she waited. She shivered despite the warm lining, for it was a chilly morning in early March. Occasional remnants of snow dotted the stone path and beds, and the bare stalks of the climbing roses rubbed against the garden wall.

She wondered if she should have come here at all. Perhaps she should have stayed in her chamber, where her uncle believed her to be.

She should have been engaged in her prayers, instead of sitting in a barren garden awaiting a young man.

A very handsome, charming young man.

The first time she had set eyes on Dylan De-Lanyea, he had been standing in the courtyard among a group of other knights. They, warriors all, had turned to look at her uncle's cortege.

Her gaze had been drawn to the dark-eyed, good-looking man whose black hair brushed his shoulders. He stood with his arms casually folded, his weight on one long, lean leg.

At once she had been reminded of Lady Katherine's cautions regarding evil young men who only had one thing in mind when it came to women. The one thing was, Genevieve had to assume from Lady Katherine's tone, something a young lady should not want.

This dangerous goal had remained a mystery until that night when the older girls also fostered to Lady Katherine had taken it upon themselves to enlighten the younger ones. Certain portions of that fascinating discussion had immediately returned to Genevieve as she tried to look away from the handsome stranger with his devilish grin and merry eyes. She had not been able to manage it until her uncle barked at his men to dismount. Half-afraid and half-hopeful, she had wondered if the young man would approach her. He did not, but later she had discovered that he was Dylan DeLanyea, the nephew of Baron DeLanyea, lord of Craig Fawr.

What would her uncle say if he discovered her now, in this secluded garden, waiting for Dylan?

She could not even imagine the extent of his ire. They were guests of the DeLanyeas, breaking their journey north at the baron's castle and, incidentally, attending the knighting of the baron's youngest son. Nevertheless, she was sure her uncle would not hesitate to condemn her in front of them all if he thought her guilty of shameful behavior.

As for what Lady Katherine would say, that was easier to guess, for she had lived the past eight years under Lady Katherine's roof, being instructed in the skills, duties and manners of a chatelaine.

Lady Katherine would say that Dylan DeLanyea, for all his smiles and kind looks, was not to be trusted.

Genevieve didn't believe that. Dylan was noble and chivalrous, and completely trustworthy.

To be sure, he had kissed her, even though he knew she was betrothed. Three times. Once on the cheek, and twice on the lips.

Her heartbeat quickened. During the somewhat tedious business of the knighting of Trystan DeLanyea, Dylan's cousin and foster brother, she had realized that Dylan was looking at her—often. And smiling. He continued to do so during the subsequent feast.

And then came the dancing. She had thought she would swoon when Dylan approached her and asked her to stand beside him in the dance. When he had taken her hand, she had scarce been able to breathe.

Fortunately, thanks to Lady Katherine's teaching, she was able to dance the steps, even though she found it exceedingly difficult to concentrate.

Afterward, Dylan DeLanyea had escorted her

back to her uncle. Then he had returned and beseeched her to dance again.

That time, when the dance was over, he did not take her back to her uncle, who was engaged in deep conversation with the baron and his eldest son, Griffydd. Instead, he led her to a more private part of the hall—still in full view of everyone, of course, so there could be no charge of impropriety.

She was, after all, betrothed—albeit to a man old enough to be her father.

Her face flushed as she thought of what had happened next. Somehow, and she wasn't sure just how, she found herself farther back in the shadows. Nor could she recall what they had been speaking of, for all at once, Dylan DeLanyea had suddenly leaned forward and kissed her.

She was not cold now, as she remembered the sensation of his warm, soft lips first brushing her cheek, then touching her mouth.

"There is a rose blooming here, after all."

She started when she heard Dylan's musical Welsh voice.

She stood as he came through the gate, closing it softly behind him before he faced her, smiling.

His untamed hair moved gently in the chilly breeze. He did not look cold, although he wore no cloak. He was clad in an open-necked shirt beneath a leather tunic girded by a thick sword belt. The tunic brushed his muscular thighs, which were encased in breeches. Fur wrappings covered his shins and boots.

Plain clothing indeed, and yet he looked absolutely splendid. She did not think a prince could look finer, especially when he regarded her with that intimate smile and those shining eyes.

"I was afraid you would not come," he said as he approached her.

Genevieve looked at the frosty ground. "I should not, perhaps, have done so."

"I would have been very sad."

She risked a glance at him. "Truly?"

"Most truly. Come, sit here beside me."

He sat on the stone bench she had recently vacated. Her heart throbbing so that she was sure he must be able to hear it, she hesitated a moment, then joined him, sitting as far away as possible.

Although she had been unable to resist the lure of being alone with him in the garden, she *was* a lady, and there were certain proprieties to be observed.

But not by him, apparently, for he boldly reached out and took her gloved hand in his.

She knew she should not allow such familiarity, but the words of protest would not come.

"Baron DeLanyea tells me you are to leave tomorrow," he said softly.

She nodded.

He sighed. "I will be very sorry when you go."

Emboldened by his manner and his words, she looked at him. "So will I."

He smiled wistfully. "You are to be married within the month?"

"Yes, within the month," she replied, not troubling to hide her dismay at her impending fate. "To an old man."

"That is often the way of it," Dylan replied gravely. "An old man and a young wife."

"Why must it be so? It doesn't seem right."

She saw that her forceful words startled him. "I know such a match is not unusual, and I know my marriage to Lord Kirkheathe pleases my uncle, who is my guardian now, yet I wish I were not betrothed."

When Dylan answered, he sounded as sad as she felt, and his hand squeezed hers. "But you are."

"I wish I could stay."

"I wish you could, too," he replied softly, reaching up to caress her cheek.

"Is there nothing to be done?"

"I fear there is not, my lady. We must say our

farewells. Let us do so here, where we can be alone.''

Her eyes welled with tears. ''I do not want to say farewell.''

''Then do not,'' he whispered, bending his head to kiss her.

For a fleeting instant, it crossed Genevieve's mind that she should not allow such a liberty.

Yet she could not stop him, or herself. She wrapped her arms around him and leaned against him as she lost herself in the wonderful sensations his lips engendered.

Dylan shifted closer, moving his hands into the warmth of her cloak to hold her in his arms. He caressed her slim back as his kiss deepened.

Engulfed in the pleasure of their embrace, he let himself drift on a sea of delightful perceptions. The perfect softness of her lips. The slight arch in her back. The brush of the fur lining on the backs of his hands.

Her lips parted ever so slightly, and he needed no more invitation to push his tongue gently between them. As he did so, he moved his hand to cup the malleable flesh of her breast.

As her tongue boldly intertwined with his, she made a sound in the back of her throat, half moan, half whimper.

The small noise broke the spell, and reminded him who she was, as well as what she was.

Despite her responses, she was Lady Genevieve Perronet, the betrothed of Lord Kirkheathe, niece of stern Lord Pomphrey Perronet, and on her way to be married.

With more reluctance than he cared to acknowledge even to himself, Dylan pulled away and tried to smile as he looked at her. The corona of blond curls that clustered around her heart-shaped face was a little disheveled. Her cheeks glowed, and her bold, blue-eyed gaze seemed to transfix him and render him speechless.

As well as fill him with a burning desire.

He did not want to talk, let alone say a farewell.

He pulled her onto his lap. No tender, tentative kiss this time, but a passionate taking of her mouth. She responded with equal fervor, clutching him as if she never wanted to let go. With increasing need, he stroked and caressed her, drawing forth small moans and sighs that spurred him on, as the shifting movement of her body increased his arousal.

Usually, he preferred to take his time and linger over every delightful step on the path. Here, now, with this young woman who looked so innocent yet who kissed with such wanton abandon, he simply could not wait.

Still kissing her, he fumbled with the ties of her cloak, determined to undo it. Finally, with a low growl of both want and frustration, he tore the strings and shoved it from her shoulders. He did the same at the back of her bodice, until it was loose enough for his hands to travel inside to the warm, satiny flesh.

She gasped when he touched her, then arched, another moan breaking from her slender throat.

He kissed her there, too.

"Dylan," she whispered fervently, her breasts rising and falling rapidly. "I...I must go."

Even then, she cupped his face with her palms and pressed more kisses upon his cheek.

"Stay," he murmured, grinding his hips in response to the pressure of her buttocks.

One hand left the confines of her bodice and went to her ankle. He began to slowly push her skirt higher, his hand running up her slim bare leg.

He had to possess her.

The bell that summoned the servants to the evening meal began to ring.

Dylan went still as a stone when he realized what he had been about to do. With a betrothed lady. In his aunt's rose garden.

He had not even intended to kiss her. He had

thought only to say a brief and suitably touching farewell in the garden before this evening's feast.

He had meant every word he said to Griffydd. His flirtation with Genevieve Perronet was just that: a flirtation. A bit of meaningless fun while they were at Craig Fawr.

He simply had not been prepared for the startling intensity in her eyes as she had looked at him, or the extreme sadness in her voice as she spoke of leaving. Nor had he at all anticipated the fire of passion in her willing kiss.

Anwyl, he, a man who had been intimate with a number of women and fathered children by some of them, had never guessed shy, demure Genevieve Perronet possessed the power to be so astonishingly arousing.

Appalled by his lack of self-control, he gently pushed her off his lap and stood. "Forgive me, my lady."

Her hair more disheveled than ever, her lips swollen from his kisses, her cheeks red and her bodice loose about her body, she regarded him with obvious confusion.

He tugged his tunic back into place, then strode to the gate. His hand on the latch, he paused and glanced back, to see that Genevieve had pulled her cloak around her shoulders.

"Farewell," he said softly, and then he opened the gate and left her.

That evening at the feast, Genevieve anxiously searched for Dylan DeLanyea. She had to be subtle about it, for her uncle was sitting beside her. Although her hawklike relative seemed most interested in discussing matters of state with the other nobles around him, he was not ignoring her.

The comfortable hall was filled with fine and titled men and their wives, both Norman and Welsh: the Baron DeGuerre, Sir Urien Fitzroy, Sir Hu Morgan, Sir Roger de Montmorency, to name but a few. Their host was quite well-known in his own right, and rather fearsome to look at, Genevieve thought, with his scarred face, one eye and limping gait.

The women of Craig Fawr were friendly and seemed quite nice, except perhaps for Griffydd DeLanyea's bride. Seona was with child again, and it seemed she was having a difficult time. Perhaps that was due to the fact that her second pregnancy came so hard upon her first, for her infant son was not yet a year old. Still, Genevieve envied her the children, and looked forward to the day she would be a mother.

She also envied her hostess, who seemed to be

everything that Lady Katherine said a chatelaine should be: kind, competent, pleasant. Everything at Craig Fawr was well-regulated and comfortable, too. Genevieve sighed and hoped that she would be so successful when it was her time to take on such duties.

The center of most people's attention tonight, however, was Trystan DeLanyea. Like all the DeLanyea men, he was comely. He shared Dylan's dark, curling hair, worn to his shoulders in the manner of his father, brother and cousin, so that altogether, they reminded Genevieve of a band of savage Celts. Trystan also shared Dylan's sensual lips, although he did not smile as much. He lacked his cousin's snapping black eyes, possessing instead the grave, gray eyes of his older brother.

So, Genevieve mused as she regarded him, he was young and handsome, but he did not fascinate her, not as Dylan did.

She had been rather astonished to think that Dylan was not already married, but perhaps, she thought with a secret, satisfied smile, he had never met the right woman before.

She wondered where he was. She knew he was still at Craig Fawr. She would have heard if he had ridden out, for he came with a troop of ten men, although his own castle, Beaufort, was not very far away.

It had to be love she felt for him, she told herself. She seemed to melt whenever he looked at her with his passionate dark eyes, and when he kissed her...there were no words to describe what she felt then.

And he must love her, too, to embrace her as he had in the garden.

Of course, they had perhaps gone a little far, but that only proved that he returned her love. He had looked so sorry when he stopped and even more when he said farewell. If he did not come to the feast, she didn't doubt it was because he thought their situation hopeless, since she was betrothed to Lord Kirkheathe.

"We will leave at first light," her uncle said beside her, momentarily drawing her attention away from her silent search. "Be ready."

"Yes, Uncle."

"The journey to Lord Kirkheathe's estates should take a sennight."

Genevieve nodded her head—then her heart seemed to stop, for Dylan *was* there, seated half-hidden by a pillar in the vast hall. No wonder she had not been able to see him before.

Looking at Dylan, she knew she could never

marry Lord Kirkheathe now. She started to raise her hand in greeting, then glanced at her uncle.

Better, perhaps, if she made no sign.

Despite her conviction, her uncle was an ambitious, unsympathetic man who would never understand her feelings—but something had to be done to prevent her arranged marriage.

Again, her gaze strayed toward the dark-haired warrior. Even his smile was enough to make her heart race and her mind recall how his lips felt upon her own.

Her breath caught in her throat as he looked her way, but he did not meet her gaze. Instead, he turned away, a slightly troubled frown on his handsome face.

Because he was as upset as she was at the possibility of her marriage to another, Genevieve didn't doubt. He must feel it too painful even to look at her.

Yes, something had to be done to prevent her marriage to Lord Kirkheathe. Dylan, being an honorable man, would not seek to do so.

She, therefore, must, she decided.

She, therefore, would.

Chapter Two

"**B**y God, I'll kill you!"

Still half-asleep and completely naked, Dylan rolled over and stared at the enraged Lord Perronet at the door of his bedchamber.

The man's face was as red as a cherry and—most surprising of all—he was fumbling for the sword at his side.

Now wide-awake, Dylan reached for his own weapon, which should have been beside his bed. He halted in stunned shock as his hand encountered an unexpected mound.

That moved.

"Uncle?" Genevieve Perronet said as she sat up, holding the coverings over herself.

It was obvious that beneath those coverings, she was as naked as he.

"Anwyl!" he cried. "What—?"

"Varlet! Churl! I'm going to kill you for what you've done!" Lord Perronet roared, finally succeeding in drawing his sword.

Realizing the man seriously intended to attack him, Dylan leapt from the bed and frantically searched for his weapon.

What had he done with it last night?

What had he done last night, period!

He spotted his sword belt slung over the chair in the corner and lunged for it as Lord Perronet charged toward him.

Genevieve screamed. Dylan grabbed his sheath and drew his sword, whirling around and jumping out of the way of Perronet's blow without a moment to spare.

"Stop! Uncle, please! Stop!" Genevieve cried.

"Quiet, woman!" Perronet bellowed.

Dylan crouched in a defensive stance, ignoring Genevieve and keeping his gaze firmly on his opponent. He could tell Lord Perronet had not wielded a sword in some time. Nevertheless, even an unskilled man could be dangerous with a heavy broadsword.

"Dylan, my love, don't hurt him!"

Dylan glanced at Genevieve, then back to her

enraged uncle. "Put up your sword, my lord, for I warn you, I will defend myself."

"You defiler of women! Base, despicable lout!" Perronet shouted. "I should have known! Your father was the same, and his father before him!"

A muscle in Dylan's jaw started to twitch. "Be careful what you say to me, old man. I don't want to hurt you, but I'll kill you if you insult me again."

"It is you who have insulted the honor of my family!" Perronet cried. "*Your* family hasn't had any honor in a hundred years!"

"Shut it, Perronet, or God help me, I'll run you through!"

"Dylan! Uncle!"

"Do you think everyone's forgotten about your lout of a father, you bastard?" Perronet snarled as they circled each other. "We all know the stories of his rapes and thievery and dishonor! A scoundrel from a line of scoundrels—and you are just the same!"

With a bellow like an angry bear, Dylan lifted his sword to strike.

"Please, don't!" Genevieve shouted.

Dylan hesitated at her distressed plea, and in that moment, Perronet moved out of range of Dylan's blow.

"What in the name of God is going on?" Baron DeLanyea demanded from the door.

The combatants ignored the baron and continued to circle each other warily.

"Baron DeLanyea!" Genevieve cried, relieved by his presence, for surely her uncle and the man she loved would not come to blows if the baron interceded.

The baron looked at her, the brow over his remaining eye rising with surprise, and she modestly pulled the bedclothes up to her chin.

She had been expecting some kind of confrontation between her uncle and Dylan. That was necessary—but she had never imagined that her uncle would try to kill him.

"I said," the baron repeated in a voice as firm and cold as iron, "what is going on?"

"Your nephew has seduced my niece!" Perronet replied. "That rogue of a bastard has ruined her!"

The baron ran his gaze over Genevieve again, and this time, she thought she saw something other than surprise and dismay.

Disrespect?

She flushed hotly at that notion, but told herself there was no help for it. She had to break the betrothal with Lord Kirkheathe and sneaking into Dylan's bed had seemed the easiest way.

Of course, it would not be without some damage to her reputation, but that would happen however she contrived to break the betrothal.

"Dylan, is this true?" the baron asked with amazing calm, given the circumstances.

"No! I have no idea how she came to be in my bed!"

"You do not know?"

"You lying bastard!" Perronet charged.

"Say that again, and *I will kill you*," Dylan growled.

Wrapping herself in the bedclothes, for her folded clothes were on a chest on the other side of the room, Genevieve clambered from the bed. "Please, don't fight. This can be settled—"

"Look there! What more evidence do you need?" Perronet demanded, pointing with his sword to the dried drops of blood Genevieve had squeezed from her pricked fingertip onto the bottom sheet.

"We will simply have to be married," Genevieve said.

"What?" Dylan gasped, lowering his sword and staring at her, wide-eyed with…horror?

Her stomach knotted. "Yes. You love me. I love

you. We…we spent the night together. We have to be married.''

He shook his head, his angry gaze boring into her. ''Oh, no, we don't.''

Now truly dismayed and fearful, she stammered, ''You…you kissed me…and…''

''Quiet, Genevieve!'' her uncle commanded as he marched toward the baron. ''Your nephew, who is, I understand, also your foster son, has basely used and deceived my niece. What are you going to do about it?''

''Nothing—at the moment,'' the baron replied just as calmly. ''I suggest we let them get dressed and then we can discuss this…situation…in a more rational manner.

''Without swords,'' he finished pointedly.

''She's right. They'll have to be married,'' Perronet declared. ''Lord Kirkheathe—''

The baron held up his hand, silencing him. ''Please, Lord Perronet, let us take some time to calm ourselves. Then we can decide how best to proceed.''

Her uncle hesitated, then sheathed his sword while continuing to regard Dylan disdainfully. ''Because you ask it of me, Baron, I will. But that whelp will make amends!''

With that, he reached out and grabbed Genevieve roughly by the arm.

"Come along, girl!" he growled, pulling her toward the door.

"My dress—"

"Leave it!" he snarled as he all but dragged her past the baron.

Dylan raised his sword again and took a step forward.

"Let them go," the baron commanded. "Did you hear me, Dylan? Let them go!"

"He cannot treat her that way!"

"Get dressed."

Dylan glanced down at his naked body. Without another word, he threw his sword on the bed and picked up his breeches, which were lying on the floor. He looked around for his tunic, noticing the unfamiliar clothing on the chest.

Not unfamiliar, he corrected, for he recognized the gown Genevieve had worn last evening at the banquet, when he had done his best to avoid her.

He spotted his tunic slung over the chair and yanked it on.

"No matter what she's done, he shouldn't have been so rough with her," he muttered before he stuck his head out of the garment.

"Her uncle has the right to treat her as he sees

fit," the baron replied, coming farther into the room. "What rights have you been enjoying?"

"Not that! I don't know how she got in my bed."

With a sinking heart, Dylan noted the skeptical quirk of the baron's lips as he sat in the chair. He looked like a king about to dispense judgment.

He suddenly wished the baron's wife were there. Lady Roanna's serenity would be welcome at a time like this. Unfortunately, the baron's ancient nurse was very ill; Lady Roanna had been tending to her when she was not involved in the preparations for the festivities surrounding Trystan's knighting.

"He called me a bastard, that cur," Dylan said defensively.

"You are a bastard," the baron replied evenly.

"I know that!" Dylan replied. "But he had no right to impugn my honor."

"He thinks he does, and the evidence is against you."

"Don't you think I would remember having a beauty like Genevieve Perronet in my arms?" Dylan protested, his arms akimbo. *"I didn't make love with her!"*

"Sit down," the baron ordered, pointing at the bed.

Dylan didn't like the coldness of his uncle's tone.

Nevertheless, he had been told to sit, and that was some cause for comfort. When he had been naughty as a child, he had been kept standing while he was chastised.

Of course, this situation was different from stealing apples or sneaking out of the castle at night, and he wasn't ten years old anymore.

When he was seated, the baron said, "You can see how this looks, Dylan. She was naked in your bed."

"I never touched her. At least, not last night."

The baron reached up to scratch the scar that extended beneath his brown leather eye patch. "But before then? What were you up to with Genevieve Perronet?"

"Nothing—or nothing much. I certainly never said I wanted her to break her betrothal, and God knows I never invited her to my bed. You have to believe that, Uncle. I've never seduced a woman with a promise of marriage."

"Good thing, or you would have been married at fourteen."

The baron's remark, although grimly said, made Dylan relax a little more. "I honestly have no idea how she came to be in my bed, naked or otherwise.''

''*That* is what I find most surprising of all. Is it possible you could have brought her here without remembering? Were you drunk last night?''

''I had some wine and ale, and I was very tired. But I'm certain I would have remembered making love.''

Indeed, as he recalled the perfect pale flesh of Genevieve's shoulders and the pretty tumble of her blond hair, he *knew* he would have remembered. ''She must have come into my bed after I was asleep.''

''I suppose that might be possible,'' the baron replied with a dubious expression. ''How do you explain the blood on the sheets?''

''I don't. I can't—because I don't know how it came to be there. Maybe I've got a cut someplace and it bled.''

''That's possible. Did you look?''

''Not yet.''

''Lord Perronet will no doubt want to see such a cut, if it exists.''

Dylan regarded the baron steadily. ''There was no need for him to try to kill me, or to manhandle Genevieve that way.''

''Put yourself in his place, Dylan. He manages

to get her betrothed to one of the most powerful men in the north of England, and then he finds her in your bed."

"I didn't—"

The baron nodded patiently. "I believe you. But he may not. He hardly knows you."

"He seems to know *of* me, or at least my family," Dylan replied dourly.

"Your grandfather was well-known, and your father had a certain..."

"Infamy," Dylan provided.

"Yes. So you see, he knows no good of your family. When he saw her in that bed, the poor fellow must have nearly died of shock. God's wounds, I almost did myself when I got here."

"How did he come to find us together?" Dylan asked suspiciously. "Who told him Genevieve was with me?"

"I don't think anybody did. It was rather obvious last night that she could hardly keep her eyes off you."

"I gave her no encouragement last night. I didn't dance with her, or even say a word."

"Perhaps not, but if a man finds a girl missing, and that girl is clearly attracted to a personable young man, his thoughts might tend to certain conclusions."

Dylan sighed heavily as he ran his hand through his thick hair. "That's why I tried to ignore her last night."

"Regrettably, your actions did not have the effect you intended."

The baron leaned toward him. "What happened between you before last night, Dylan? It's clear she thought if the betrothal was broken, you would wed her. Did you give her cause to think you wanted to marry her if she was free?"

Dylan smote his forehead. "God's holy heart, that's why she did it—to break the betrothal!"

"Obviously. Did you tell her that?"

"*Anwyl*, no! I said I would be sorry to see her leave or some such thing."

"What else?"

"Nothing else!"

"What else did you *do?*"

"I...there may have been some kissing," he muttered, looking at his feet.

"Kissing?"

"Passionate kissing," he confessed.

"Just kissing?"

"A little more."

"What 'little more'?"

Frustrated, Dylan raised his eyes and regarded the baron resolutely. "You're a man. You can guess. But I never made love to her, or even got close to it.''

"Dylan," the baron began not unkindly, "do you never stop to think? Lady Genevieve has been with Lady Katherine DuMonde the past eight years. I doubt she's even talked to many men that whole time. Now she's traveling to be married to a man she's never seen, and who she knows is not young. They stop here, and who does she meet but you?

"I won't be telling you anything you don't already know when I say you're as handsome a young man as she's ever likely to meet, and—" he grinned for an instant "—you've got a merry devilry that reminds me of myself at your age, so I know how attractive that quality can be.

"I do not doubt that you've grievously underestimated the effect you had on her," he continued, serious again. "She thought you liked her more than you intended, and saw a way to get out of a marriage she didn't want."

"I suppose I should have listened to Griffydd," Dylan muttered.

"What does Griffydd have to do with this?"

Dylan shrugged. "He tried to warn me, but I..."

"Yes, you should have paid attention," the baron replied. "But that is past. The question before us now is, what can we say to assuage her uncle?''

"I won't be forced to marry her just to save her honor, which *she* compromised," Dylan warned.

"You know I am not a proponent of forced marriages, for any reason," the baron replied. "We must think of a way to let the marriage to Lord Kirkheathe proceed as planned."

As the baron regarded the silent young man he had known from his birth, his brow furrowed with concern. "You do want the marriage to Kirkheathe to proceed?"

Dylan shrugged again. "Naturally. But after all the racket Lord Perronet made, her reputation may already be too seriously ruined. Kirkheathe might spurn her."

"That is true." The baron sighed.

"Unless I can convince Lord Perronet that I did not make love to his niece and so there is no reason she cannot marry Kirkheathe."

"*You* will convince him?"

Feeling a certain amount of guilt over what he had done with Genevieve, he nodded. "I will try."

"So there is no reason at all she cannot marry Kirkheathe?"

Dylan rose and faced his foster father. "If there is, it is only in her own mind."

"Or heart, perhaps."

"Perhaps," he agreed after a short silence.

"Well, then," the baron said, rising. "I suggest you waste no time. The longer Lord Perronet is on the rampage, the worse the damage to Lady Genevieve's reputation will be."

Dylan nodded and turned to go.

Before he could leave, the baron reached out and laid a hand on his shoulder. "She seems a sweet girl, if misguided. Do not fault her too much for her foolishness."

Dylan smiled his irrepressible smile. "Because she claims to be in love with me, I will be chivalry itself when I talk to her."

Then a scowl replaced the smile as he strode from the room.

"As for her uncle, I can make no such promises."

Having hastily dressed in a gown of what she considered a most appropriate black, Genevieve sat staring at her hands folded on her lap. Her uncle was going to be here at any moment, and she was doing her best to compose herself.

It was not easy. Indeed, if someone were to offer her a means of being spirited out of Craig Fawr to the farthest reaches of Europe, she would consider herself the most fortunate of beings.

Sadly, no such miraculous event was in the offing.

And yet it was not shame and sorrow that filled her heart at the moment. It was a fierce and righteous anger, because she had been tricked by a clever rogue bent only on his own amusement.

She never should have trusted Dylan DeLanyea's kisses and his smiles and his sorrowful words. She should have remembered Lady Katherine's admonitions that most young men were scheming, lustful rascals best avoided.

To think she had believed that he loved her! That his passionate kisses meant that he cared. Instead, as she had discovered to her horror and her shame, he had only been toying with her and amusing himself at her expense.

She should have been a dutiful niece and gladly gone to her marriage instead of climbing into a bed beside a naked and softly snoring Welshman who had promised her...nothing.

And she never should have cut her own finger to make it look as if she had bled. That was something one of the other girls at Lady Katherine's claimed would happen the first time she lay with a man. That girl had lost her virginity some time before to a soldier in her father's employ.

How she had looked down on Cecily Debarry after she had heard that, Genevieve thought, disgusted with herself as she remembered. That was how people would think of her now, as a sinful, immoral creature—and it was Dylan DeLanyea's fault!

"Are you dressed?" her uncle demanded from the other side of the door.

"Yes," she answered, rising and steeling herself for his anger. She would try to tell him the truth—that she was a virgin still—and her reasons for the deception, but she had little hope that he would listen.

What hope she had was squelched the moment her uncle marched into the chamber. He was still so angry, his hawklike face seemed filled with fury and his brown eyes fairly snapped with wrath as he slammed the heavy door shut.

Explanations would be useless. How could she save herself from his ire?

Quickly she knelt before him in an attitude of humble contrition, her anger masked, her head lowered, pressing her palms together as if she were praying—and she was, silently begging God to help her from this morass she had created.

"Uncle, I beg your forgiveness for my shameful conduct," she murmured contritely. "I am very sorry."

"So you should be."

Noting that he didn't sound quite so angry, she

risked a glance up at him, and thought she saw a crack in the veneer of wrath.

"I was weak and foolish."

Because I thought he loved me.

"All women are weak and foolish," her uncle growled. "It is their nature."

"I regret that I have sinned so grievously."

And trusted him.

"You could not help it, I suppose," he said, slightly mollified. "Like Eve when she was tempted by a snake."

She tentatively raised her eyes to regard him.

"I suppose the betrothal to Lord Kirkheathe must be broken?" she asked with very real remorse.

She had never met the man, did not know him—but could marriage to him make her feel any worse?

"He very specifically wanted a virgin," her uncle muttered as he strolled to the window and stared out, unseeing.

Genevieve swallowed hard. That did not make the man sound any more attractive; still, what alternatives existed?

"You will have to marry DeLanyea."

She stared at him. "After what he did?"

Her uncle turned to face her. "We have little choice."

"Lord Kirkheathe lives far away. Rumors may not reach him, so he need not know—"

Her uncle's fierce scowl silenced her. "*I* will know, and I gave the man my word that you were a virgin. Besides, Kirkheathe hears everything one way or another. Since you are no longer pure, honor demands that I break the contract, just as honor demands that DeLanyea marry you after what he has done."

"But I do not want to marry him now!"

"You wanted him enough last night to dishonor yourself," he noted, glaring at her.

"I...I was overwhelmed by him. I made a mistake. I should not have done it."

"Girl, get it through your head. Your reputation is irrevocably destroyed—unless he marries you."

She got to her feet.

"Uncle," she said resolutely, "I am a virgin still. It was a ruse to break the betrothal. I crept into his bed last night when he was already asleep."

Her uncle's eyes narrowed. "Did that bastard tell you to say that?"

"No! It is the truth. I thought he loved me and would want to marry me if I were free. Clearly, I made a serious error," she finished bitterly.

"Yes, you did," her uncle concurred grimly. "Whatever stupid thing you *thought,* this is not some childish prank, easily mended. Easily forgiven.''

It was unfortunately obvious that he did not believe her explanation.

''There is only one way out of this with even a hint of honor. You must and shall marry Dylan DeLanyea, and now I will ensure that is what comes to pass.''

He started for the door.

''I would rather die!''

He halted, then wheeled slowly on his heel to regard her dispassionately, as if she were a stranger to him. ''There is a window. Jump.''

Appalled at his cold remark, she could only stare at him.

''I thought you would not,'' he muttered as he left her.

After he closed the door, she heard the sound of a key in the lock.

Sinking down on the chair, she put her head in her hands.

And cursed herself for a fool.

Chapter Three

"My lord!" Dylan cried as he nearly collided with Lord Perronet on the steps leading to Genevieve's chamber.

"DeLanyea," the nobleman snarled, glaring at him.

Dylan tried to remain calm, or at least as calm as he had been since his abrupt waking this morning. He would rather have talked to Genevieve first, but he might as well get the worst over with, he told himself. "I would speak with you, my lord."

"Yes, you will," the man replied. "But not here."

Dylan fought to keep the scowl off his face. Of course he would not discuss this business on the stairs. "My uncle's solar would, perhaps, be best."

"Show me the way."

Without a word, Dylan turned on his heel. He led the man down the stairs and through the hall, ignoring his uncle and cousins as they sat breaking the fast, to a tower recently built abutting the hall. The lower levels were used as offices by the steward and the bailiff. The baron's solar was on the second level, and a fine new bedchamber for the baron and his wife comprised the third.

He waited for Lord Perronet to enter the room, then followed him, closing the door behind him.

"Please, sit," he offered, gesturing at the baron's chair behind the large wooden table.

"I prefer to stand."

Dylan shrugged, then he himself took the baron's chair. At that, Lord Perronet looked even more irate, but Dylan didn't much care. If the man insisted upon standing, so that now he looked like a humble penitent brought before the lord of the manor, he had only himself to blame.

Like his niece.

"You've dishonored her, so you've got to marry her," Lord Perronet declared without further preamble.

"I did not, so I do not," Dylan replied. "I don't know what she told you, but I didn't even know she was in my bed until you came barging into my chamber this morning. If there's dishonor here, you cannot lay it at my feet.''

"It's not your feet that ruined her," Lord Perronet growled. "She was in your bed with blood on the sheets, man! That's evidence enough for what you did.''

"That is evidence that somebody bled for some reason. Otherwise, it is my word against hers.''

"The word of my niece against that of a—''

"Bastard?'' Dylan regarded him steadily. "I must say, my lord, I'm surprised you would insist I marry her, given your low opinion of my family.''

"You gave me no choice." The nobleman's brows lowered. "Perhaps that was your plan—to get her dowry as well as entry into my family.''

"If I did dishonor her, as you claim, those would be the furthest things from my mind. I don't need her dowry, and I certainly don't want to be related to you in any way.''

The nobleman's frown deepened. "Then why did you do it? To destroy my allegiance with Kirkheathe?''

"I don't give a fisherman's fart for your allegiances," Dylan retorted. "That's a Norman for you, thinking only of power and gain.''

"You young—''

"Welshman," Dylan interrupted.

If the man insulted him again, he was quite likely to lose what remained of his control over his temper, and that would be a mistake.

"Or rather," Dylan continued, "happily more Welsh than Norman. Tell me, my lord, what does the lady say? Does she claim that I made love to her under promise of marriage?"

Lord Perronet didn't hesitate a moment. "Yes."

The bile rose in Dylan's throat. Genevieve had lied as blatantly as any charlatan, making him bear the blame.

"She is but a weak-willed girl easily led astray by a honey-tongued young man."

Dylan thought of Genevieve's eyes before his passionate kiss.

She was no weak-willed girl; she was a woman, with a woman's passion.

And a very adult capacity to lie without detection.

He rose and faced Lord Perronet. "Whatever I may or may not have done, I will not be blackmailed into marriage."

For the first time, it finally seemed to penetrate Lord Perronet's brain that Dylan could not be compelled to marry Genevieve under these, or perhaps any, circumstances.

"I hope you realize you've destroyed her chances," he snarled. "There'll be nothing for her but a convent—a secluded one."

"That is not my concern."

"No, it isn't, is it?" Perronet demanded. "Just like your father, aren't you? Don't think about consequences—just so long as you get what you want! Greedy to the bone!"

"If you were wise, you would cut out your tongue before you spoke of my father again," Dylan said quietly as he came out from behind the table.

Lord Perronet's eyes filled with panic, and he took a step back.

"I am not the greedy one here, my lord," Dylan continued in that same softly menacing tone. "What will *you* forfeit if the betrothal between your niece and Kirkheathe is broken? Money? Power? Influence? All three? Was there ever any thought of *her* happiness when you made that betrothal?"

Lord Perronet stepped back again as Dylan approached him like a lion stalking its prey. "Perhaps if you had thought of her, she would not have been driven to impugn my honor to avoid marrying against her will."

"I...she..."

"You would sacrifice her happiness for your greed," he accused.

"You...you impertinent—!" Lord Perronet spluttered.

"Watch your tongue, my lord! Or should I say, Uncle?"

The man's eyes widened.

"Why look so surprised? Isn't that what you came here demanding, that I should marry your niece? *Anwyl,* maybe I should. She wanted me, after all, so there is that to consider. And you are a rich, powerful man."

"You wouldn't dare!" Lord Perronet gasped.

"You seem to think I am capable of anything. Why not honorable marriage? Tell me, my lord, what might her dowry be?"

"It is—it doesn't matter what it is! You will never see it!"

"This may be an appropriate time to point out that my own family is not insignificant," Dylan said. "While I agree my father and grandfather were despicable monsters, my uncle and his sons are considered among the finest nobles in all of England. Baron DeLanyea is easily a match for you in powerful friends, as well as wealth. So you see, my haughty Norman, perhaps marriage to me is not to be considered a fate only slightly better than life in a secluded convent.

"Now, I ask you again, what is the lady's dowry?"

Baron DeLanyea glanced at the entrance to the tower containing his solar, then back to the bread and ale before him as he broke the fast.

"God's wounds, nerve-racking this is, and no mistake," he muttered to his sons, who sat on either side of him.

"If he doesn't part the man's head from his body, it will be a miracle," Griffydd observed.

"Then someone should go and make sure he doesn't," Trystan said, looking pointedly at his father.

"He won't attack the man," the baron said, although not without the merest hint of doubt in his voice. "He wouldn't be that stupid."

"He hasn't proved to be very wise these days," Griffydd remarked.

"That is true enough."

Trystan stood abruptly. "Someone should see what they're doing."

"Sit down," the baron ordered. "If we have to interfere, we will—but not unless it's absolutely necessary."

"He'll make things worse, and hasn't he done enough harm already?"

"He says he has not," the baron reminded his younger son.

"I saw the way he looked at her," Trystan replied. He looked at Griffydd. "You did, too. I know you spoke to him about his behavior."

"And I thought he had taken heed."

"He says he did," the baron said. "He didn't even talk to her at the banquet last night, did he?"

"That doesn't mean he's innocent," Trystan charged.

"I know," the baron replied. "But let us not be casting blame where it isn't deserved."

Suddenly, the older man straightened. "Shh! Someone's coming from the solar now."

All three watched expectantly as Lord Perronet strode out of the tower, through the hall and outside.

They exchanged puzzled glances.

"At least he's not dead," Griffydd offered.

"He looked angry, though," Trystan noted warily. "What do you suppose—?"

They fell silent as Dylan appeared, his head bowed as if lost in thought, a scowl on his usually smiling face until he looked up and saw his relatives.

Then he grinned, but all realized there was no true joy in it. "Congratulate me, gentlemen. I am to be married."

Griffydd and Trystan stared openmouthed as the baron slowly got to his feet. "What are you saying?"

"I am saying I am going to marry Genevieve Perronet. Today."

The baron sat back down heavily.

"Why?" Griffydd demanded, eyeing him sternly. "You claim you did not dishonor her."

Finally, a spark of mirth appeared in Dylan's dark eyes. "Maybe it is because I am of an age to be married."

"Are you certain this is a wise decision?" the baron asked. "Lord Perronet didn't force—?"

"Him? Force me to do anything?" Dylan scoffed. "That would be something to see."

"What about Lady Genevieve?" Trystan demanded.

"It was her idea, wasn't it, although she went about letting me know that she wanted to be my wife in a rather unusual way," he replied.

He turned to the baron. "You yourself heard her confess that she loved me, Uncle. Obviously, she is an intelligent woman and no one can deny her beauty."

"You are absolutely certain about this?" the baron asked.

"Uncle, do you honestly believe I could be forced by any man—or woman, either—to marry against my will?"

"No," the baron admitted.

"Griffydd?"

"No," he agreed.

"Trystan?"

"No," the youngest knight grudgingly concurred. His gaze mirrored the intensity of his father's. "Do *you* love *her?*"

"Not yet, but I shall, beginning this very night. Now if you will all excuse me, I had better start arranging my wedding."

He marched from the hall, whistling a jaunty tune as if he got married every day, leaving the other three feeling like men who had been expecting a pitched battle, only to find themselves sent home without so much as a glimpse of the enemy.

Below the table, Trystan's hands balled into fists.

Genevieve stared at her uncle in disbelief. "My *what?*"

"Your wedding dress. Get it out and get it ready. You are going to be married today."

"Married? To whom?"

He gave her a sour look. "To whom do you think? Sir Dylan DeLanyea, lord of Beaufort, that's who."

"But what of my betrothal to Lord Kirkheathe?"

"That is obviously at an end, thanks to you. I shall find some means to make amends. Maybe your cousin Elizabeth can be persuaded to marry him in your stead."

"Uncle!"

Genevieve rose from her chair and faced him resolutely. "I admit I made a grievous error, but I will not compound it by marrying that man."

"Oh, yes, you will!" her uncle replied harshly. "How dare you refuse? After what you did, you should be glad we've got a way out of it before your reputation is totally sullied. There will be rumors and gossip enough as it is. As for what Lord Kirkheathe might think, I don't want to even consider. You should thank God I'm not sending you off without a shift to your name."

"I would prefer that fate to marriage to Dylan DeLanyea."

Her uncle looked at her as if she had gone mad, and clearly he thought she had. "You were in his bed *naked*, Genevieve!"

"To my everlasting regret. I would rather marry Lord Kirkheathe."

"That's impossible, and you know it! Marry DeLanyea, or so help me, I'll send you to the most remote convent I can find and leave you there to rot!"

As she looked at his angry visage, she knew he would do exactly that. She would be exiled to an existence little better than a living death, with no husband and no possibility of children.

"Lord Perronet?"

Genevieve started and looked at the door, where the baron's wife stood.

Lady Roanna was tall and slim, dressed in a simple gown of fine red wool girdled with a belt of soft beige leather. Her hair was covered by a red cap and white scarf.

She regarded them placidly, her pale, patient face showing signs of weariness, yet her voice, while soft, was as commanding as the baron's.

Genevieve quickly curtsied. As she did so, she glanced at her proud and pompous uncle. He looked as humble and contrite as an errant child.

"Lord Perronet, I have been informed of my nephew's impending marriage and would like to speak to your niece alone, if I may. One woman to another, as it were."

When she spoke, her voice and expression were such that Genevieve doubted anyone would deny whatever request she cared to make, even including the king.

And as if to prove Genevieve's observation, her uncle nodded, meek as a lamb.

"Of course, my lady," he said. He went to the door, then hesitated, glancing back at Genevieve. "The ceremony will be at noon."

After he was gone, Lady Roanna glided into the room.

"May I sit?" she asked, and Genevieve couldn't help but be relieved by the change in her tone. She sounded much more sympathetic.

"Of course, my lady," Genevieve replied.

Lady Roanna took a chair and then gestured at the other. "Please."

Genevieve did as she was bid.

Lady Roanna turned her vibrant green eyes onto Genevieve, eyes that seemed to demand truthfulness. "So, you are going to marry my nephew, not Lord Kirkheathe."

"I have been told I must," Genevieve replied, and not without a hint of bitterness.

"You do not sound pleased."

Genevieve didn't answer. She couldn't, not with Lady Roanna's steadfast gaze on her.

"I gather your uncle has good reason for demanding this change."

"I was in your nephew's bed."

Lady Roanna's expression altered ever so slightly and in a manner that made Genevieve flush. "Dylan denies seducing you."

All Genevieve could do was stare at the floor and blush like a child caught in an outrageous lie.

"Did he seduce you?" Lady Roanna asked gently.

Compelled by the older woman's sympathy, Genevieve raised her eyes and shook her head. "No, my lady. And so I told my uncle."

Lady Roanna smiled a little. "I see. I gather this was a plan on your part to avoid marriage to Lord Kirkheathe?"

Genevieve felt her eyes welling with hot tears as she nodded. Suddenly, she felt silly and stupid and ashamed.

"Then I would say you have succeeded admirably. But tell me, were you not consulted about the betrothal to Lord Kirkheathe? Did you not agree?"

"No, my lady. That is," Genevieve amended, "I did not openly disagree. I thought I had no other choice, until I met Dylan." Her voice quivered. "I suppose you think I have behaved disgracefully."

The older woman reached out and pressed her hand warmly. "I think you have acted like a desperate young woman who believes herself in love. However, I must say I am surprised you are not happier at the prospect of marrying my nephew, since you must have suspected this would be the ultimate result of your scheme. Perhaps you have heard things about his family that have upset you?"

Although they had not been uppermost in her mind, Genevieve remembered the epithets her uncle had hurled at Dylan and his hostile reaction. "I know my uncle thinks very poorly of his father and grandfather, but I do not know why."

Lady Roanna sighed deeply. "Dylan's father and grandfather were selfish, cruel, vindictive men who craved power. They did terrible things trying to attain it. Thankfully Dylan is not like them."

"My uncle called him a bastard."

"He is. His mother was a servant girl at Beaufort."

Genevieve frowned, confused. "Yet he has inherited that estate?"

"Yes." Lady Roanna made a wry little smile. "The Welsh are not as concerned with legitimacy, and it is a good thing, too, or my husband would not be lord of Craig Fawr. He is a bastard, too."

"Oh, my lady, I'm sorry. I didn't know."

"There is no need to apologize. I just thought you might hold Dylan's birth against him."

"No, that is not what I hold against him," she replied.

She mustered her pride. "I was most unhappily misled, my lady. I thought he loved me."

"Why?"

Genevieve was not quite prepared for the blunt question, but if Lady Roanna wanted to know, she would tell her. "He was very kind and pleasant, and flattering. No man has ever looked at me as he did. And then he kissed me, more than once, with great passion. And when he said farewell…"

Her words trailed off into an awkward silence, for if she said more, she would perhaps reveal too much of her own wounded feelings, and that her pride would not allow.

"I understand he never told you that he loved you and wanted to marry you."

"No, my lady. But his embraces were…they gave me some cause to think he cared for me."

"Dylan is a passionate man," Lady Roanna observed. "He sometimes acts without much thought."

"Did he agree to marry me because my uncle forced him?" Genevieve demanded suspiciously.

Lady Roanna smiled. "If I did not know Dylan better, my dear," she admitted, "I might think that. But I do know him. No one could force him to do such a thing."

"Then why did he change his mind and say he would marry me?"

"I honestly don't know," Lady Roanna replied. "But he does seem very determined to do it." She leaned forward, her gaze searching Genevieve's face. "What I must know is, do you want to be his wife? If you do not, tell me. Neither my husband nor I believe in forced marriages."

A strange look crossed Lady Roanna's face. "For very good reasons. So, if you would rather not marry Dylan, just say so and it will not be."

"My uncle threatens to send me away to a remote convent if I do not," Genevieve replied warily.

"We would convince him otherwise."

Despite Lady Roanna's calm conviction, Genevieve found it difficult to believe they would be able to change her stubborn uncle's mind.

So now it was up to her to decide: marry Dylan DeLanyea, who only hours ago had made it very clear that he did not want her for his wife.

Or be sent to a convent, forever unmarried and childless.

Chapter Four

Somewhere in the dim recesses of Dylan's mind, he had always known he would marry one day. He had, however, envisioned doing so under distinctly different circumstances.

Whenever he had taken a moment to contemplate his future spouse, for example, he had pictured a spirited Welsh woman of voluptuous build who would understand about his children and the women who had borne them.

He had certainly never imagined himself married to a pale, blond girl-woman of Norman blood, especially one who had tricked her way into his bed, he reflected as he stood in the hall with his relatives, along with the baron's assembled guests and the castle servants.

They were all awaiting the arrival of his bride and the blessing of a priest hastily summoned.

He had also naturally assumed he would be passionately in love with his bride, a passion beyond anything he had ever felt for the many and various women who had already shared his affection and his bed.

Genevieve Perronet was attractive, of course, and she had been arousing—but he did not love her. *Anwyl,* he hardly knew her.

And therein, of course, lay the biggest problem. Angry and frustrated, he had proposed a marriage with scarcely a thought of the bride-to-be, his primary motive being to annoy her haughty, pompous uncle.

At least Genevieve would be pleased, he consoled himself, his natural optimism reasserting itself. She would be grateful that he was marrying her and saving her damaged honor.

And she *had* said she loved him.

A grateful, loving wife with a dowry of five hundred gold coins was not something to be dismissed out of hand. As for his children, he would simply have to explain to her that the Welsh were not so hypocritical when it came to illegitimate children. In Welsh eyes, a child was a child, whether born in wedlock or not.

If he and Genevieve had a son, that firstborn son would inherit Beaufort according to Norman law.

Trefor, his eldest son out of wedlock, would be given his own land out of that estate, as would his other bastard son, Arthur, equal to that of any subsequent issue.

Genevieve would simply have to accept that.

The baron, standing beside him, shifted, drawing Dylan's attention from his own musings. Glancing around the hall, Dylan realized the guests and servants were exchanging wary glances.

"Brides are often late," the baron muttered. "Wanting to look their best, is all. You know how women are."

Dylan nodded. Yes, he knew women, and so he would be patient. "Will Lady Roanna be here for the blessing?"

"Old Mamaeth is very bad but—" the baron started to explain when suddenly there was a commotion at the entrance to the hall.

Dylan found himself holding his breath, then, when he saw the reason for the disturbance, letting it out slowly.

It was Lady Roanna and the baron's old nurse, who was being carried in, seated on a chair borne by two brawny servants as if she were an Oriental potentate.

"Not missing this," the elderly woman chirped cheerfully. "It's about time that young devil settled down and got married and quit sowing his seed all over Wales.''

Dylan tried to smile. He was happy Mamaeth had made the effort to see him wed, of course, and happier yet to see Lady Roanna, who was like a mother to him.

But Mamaeth had a tongue that wagged, especially when she was in a celebratory mood, and no sense of propriety at all.

Which she proceeded to demonstrate.

''Where's the bride?'' she demanded querulously. ''Not changed her mind, I hope, after all the uproar! Nearly stopped my heart, that.''

The people in the hall smiled, but the smiles were a little strained.

''It is a good thing she is taking her time,'' Dylan replied with a merriment he didn't quite feel. ''Otherwise you would have been late.''

''Humph!'' was all the answer Mamaeth could think to make to that before she subsided into an uncharacteristic silence, and for that, Dylan was grateful.

''Ah, here they are!'' the baron cried softly.

Again Dylan looked at the entrance to the hall—and then gasped with delight.

Genevieve wore a gown of white silk whose long cuffs, lined with gold samite, reached nearly to the floor. Over this was a tunic, also of gold. Her girdle of gold and silver embroidery encircled her slender waist, crossed in back and was knotted again in front, so that it fell low on her hips.

Her hand on her stern uncle's arm, she slowly approached the group waiting on the dais, and as she did, her low-slung girdle seemed to highlight the graceful sensuality of her walk.

Surprisingly aroused, especially given the crowd surrounding him, Dylan swallowed hard and forced himself to look at her face. On her head was a stiffened band with matching embroidery held in place by a white silken scarf that passed from one side of the crown under her chin to the other.

Without the cluster of golden curls that usually surrounded her face, she looked older, and more womanly.

His heart beat faster.

Then she came near enough for him to get a good look at her expression.

Rarely had he ever seen anyone, including Griffydd, appear so grimly resolute. She looked more like a condemned prisoner being led to the block than a woman who had connived to bring about her own marriage.

If she did not want to be married to him, why was she there?

Confused, and with his pride wounded—for never had he imagined his bride would have such a look on her face—he glanced at Lady Roanna. He knew she had spoken with Genevieve. Perhaps Genevieve had given his foster mother some inkling...?

Lady Roanna smiled tranquilly, as if this were nothing more than a joyous occasion and she glad to be there.

Surely she would not look so calm if she thought there was trouble in the offing.

Next, Dylan glanced at the baron, who had a somewhat troubled frown on his face, and his sons likewise.

Dylan grew aware of the puzzled murmurs of the assembly, and the various expressions of the guests, who generally seemed to be regarding him with a certain questioning gravity, and Genevieve with...pity?

Anwyl, this was her doing. Her fault. The result of her scheming and trickery. He would have no one think this was being forced on her!

Or him, either, his pride reminded him.

So Dylan left the dais and approached his beautiful, scheming bride. When he reached her, he yanked her into his arms, and boldly and passionately kissed her.

* * *

Dylan's unexpected kiss quite took Genevieve's breath away—and threatened to strip her of what dignity she retained in front of all these people.

Try as she might to feel nothing, or perhaps only anger, the moment his lips were on hers, her blood began to throb wildly, and her knees felt strangely weak.

Finally he stopped kissing her, although he still held her in a grip of iron. His lips trailed across her cheek toward her ear while she tried to catch her breath.

"This was more your doing than mine, my lady, so smile," he whispered harshly, "or by God, I'll walk away and leave you here."

Passionate kiss or no passionate kiss, she knew he meant it. He would do it. He would see her humiliated yet again, and he would probably have the gall to say she had only herself to blame.

But she was not the one responsible for their current plight. She had refused to marry him until her uncle made his threat.

If Dylan deserted her here, after all that had passed, she would surely be sent to that convent.

Therefore, she managed to put a smile on her face and did not flinch when he possessively took hold of her hand and led her toward the baron.

The older man stepped toward them and she felt the force of his piercing, one-eyed gaze as he looked at them.

"Is this what you want, Lady Genevieve?" he asked quietly, so that only she and Dylan could hear.

"Yes," she whispered, resigned to her fate. She did not look at Dylan who was, appropriately enough, attired all in black.

"Dylan?"

"Of course."

Despite their assertions, a worried look passed over the baron's face and he glanced at his wife, who nodded. He sighed and stepped back.

"Father," he said, summoning the priest.

The priest, a bland, beatific smile on his round face, bustled forward.

"Do you have a ring, my son?" he asked kindly of Dylan.

Genevieve's bridegroom nodded and from his belt produced a thick gold band. The priest took it and made the sign of the cross over it. Then he returned it to Dylan.

"Put it on her finger," he prompted.

Genevieve held out her trembling hand. Dylan took it in his warm, callused one and placed the ring on her finger.

As he slipped it into place, the priest intoned, "In the name of the Father, and of the Son and of the Holy Ghost, may God bless this union. May you be fruitful and multiply. May no man seek to come between you. I now pronounce that you are husband and wife in the eyes of God and all here."

The hall erupted with applause and joyful cries of good wishes.

Genevieve steeled herself for another kiss from her new husband.

Which did not come, for he turned away, demanding congratulations from all and sundry, not the whit upset, it seemed, that his bride was less than overjoyed.

That Genevieve believed he was not upset was a compliment to Dylan's facility for appearing cheerful when he was not in that particular humor. In truth, he was far from pleased with the situation; however, he would have died before he would have revealed that to anyone in Craig Fawr.

Therefore, as the celebrations of the unexpected nuptials progressed, Dylan made merry. He entertained those around him with jokes, songs and stories, and gave his bride such attention as he thought he should, so that no one suspected this marriage was not to his liking.

As for what Genevieve was thinking and feeling, he told himself that was not important at present. When they were alone, when he was with her, when it was time to claim his right as her husband, then he would care.

At last the moment arrived for the bride to retire. With suitable jokes and husbandly leers, Dylan sent her off with the women.

Apparently it was necessary for several maidservants to accompany Genevieve to the bedchamber. She didn't think so; however, she said nothing, expecting them to leave her at the threshold.

They did not. Instead, they followed her inside the large room in the tower, bustling about, talking, laughing and distracting Genevieve from her surroundings.

She tried to tell them to go, but her request only seemed to inspire them to give her meaningful and lewd glances, and engender more giggles and whispered words in their native tongue.

Finally, Genevieve decided to ignore them and to scrutinize her bedchamber.

There was a table holding a basin and ewer, a candle stand filled with lighted beeswax candles, another small table bearing a carafe of wine and two silver goblets, and the bed.

The very big bed, with luxurious satin coverings.

Turning away from this extravagant piece of furniture, Genevieve heard Dylan's name mentioned yet again, followed by more riotous giggling. The faces of the youngest girls flushed brightly, even as their eyes sparkled with merriment.

Then one of them started to search in Genevieve's baggage. Before Genevieve could order her to stop, the girl triumphantly pulled out Genevieve's finest shift, which had been intended for her wedding night.

This was her wedding night.

She snatched it away. Blushing and hating herself for doing so, she said sternly and as if they were hard of hearing, "While I hate to end your enjoyment, I do not require any further assistance."

They looked at her with all the comprehension of a flock of sheep.

"Go!" she commanded, pointing at the door.

The women were obviously startled by her tone as much as her order, but Genevieve didn't care. She wanted them—and their smiles and Welsh whispers and lewd laughter—gone.

The women exchanged wary glances and moved toward the door. After they had reluctantly gone out, Genevieve closed it forcefully behind them.

If she had had a key, she would have been tempted to lock it.

Unfortunately, she did not.

Without the presence of the servants, which gave her some reason to act dignified, she felt all her trepidation and dismay returning. What she could expect from Dylan now, she did not know, nor did she particularly wish to find out.

But how could she avoid him? He was her lawful husband. He had every right...

Every right.

Flushing hotly, she looked at the fine bed with its rich coverings as she considered the intimacy she was legally bound to share with him.

She had already been intimate with him, in one way. Her body warmed as she recalled the sight of him naked as he faced her enraged uncle.

That Dylan had a body of which no man would be ashamed was without question. Tall, taut-muscled, his shoulders were broad, his waist and hips narrow. A slender band of dark hair started near his waist and moved lower, where that hair was thick and curling, too.

Everything about him was impressive.

She suddenly wondered what he would make of her body.

Not that it mattered, for she was as irrevocably

his wife as he was her husband. And soon he would be here. They would be alone. He would take her to that bed and...

She frowned studiously. She did not know what the full nature of the nuptial duties of a wife were. Unfortunately, no one had ever taken it upon themselves to tell her. All the information she had had come via whispers in the dark at Lady Katherine's.

She knew there must be blood—not a lot, but some—and also pain. His manhood must enter her...somewhere. She thought she knew where, although one or two of the girls had dissented from the general opinion by claiming it was the navel. The worldly Cecily had scoffed at that, yet they had clung to that notion so steadily, Genevieve was not ready to discount their opinion entirely.

Taking a deep breath to calm her racing heart, she went to her chest. The contents had obviously been packed in haste when it was necessary to move her belongings from her former quarters to Dylan's bedchamber, and that woman rooting through them had not helped. At last, however, she found her hairbrush.

She sat on the stool and began to brush her hair, thinking this would calm her. It took even less time to disabuse her of this notion than it had taken to find the brush.

Once the men below realized that the maidservants had been dismissed, how long would it be before Dylan came to her?

With trembling fingers she removed her gown and linen shift to put on the silken one. Looking around the room again, she wondered if some wine would help calm her. She didn't want her trepidation to be obvious.

She poured out half a goblet, regarded it, then filled it nearly to the brim. Her hands shaking, she raised it to her lips and sipped.

It was excellent wine.

She drank deeply, emptying the goblet, and felt the tension ease from her body. Indeed, she even began to feel quite...pleasant.

No wonder men drank to excess, if this floating sensation were the usual result.

She poured another goblet, pleased to note that her hands were not trembling. The carafe slipped a little as she set it down, but did not spill.

She drained this goblet, too, although not so quickly as the first. Realizing in a drowsy sort of way that she was feeling rather too warm, she stumbled a little as she made her way to the candle stand.

"Whoops!" she cried softly, giggling as she

righted herself. "You are a married lady now, Genevieve, so we must have dignity."

She stared hard at the shimmering candles, which wavered most oddly.

"Perhaps they are bewitched," she proposed aloud. "No matter."

After several tries, she managed to blow out all save one of the candles, so that the room was nearly completely dark.

She straightened. The whole room was wavering, or maybe it was just her, for it seemed there was something the matter with her legs.

"I'm just tired," she said thickly. "Very, very tired. And I don't care where he is, or what he's doing."

Holding her head high, she took a rather circuitous route to the bed, and then tried to climb into it.

It was very high, that bed, but she finally succeeded, flopping down on it and promptly falling into a deep and dreamless sleep.

Sometime later, Dylan threw himself in a chair beside Trystan. He reached out and grabbed Trystan's drinking horn, taking a long pull of rich wine and momentarily ignoring the younger man's peeved expression.

He set it down and wiped his lips with the back of his hand. "Going to begrudge me a drink, are you? You look as sour as an old woman with bad teeth."

"Are you wanting to be drunk on your wedding night?" Trystan demanded.

"What, drunk from that? Not likely, and I will be more than able to do what a husband should with a bride like that, boy."

"Don't call me 'boy.'"

Dylan leaned back to regard the young knight. "Well, well, well, all grown-up, eh? Who was it used to go crying to his mam when I wouldn't let him play with me?"

"That was a long time ago."

"So it was, so it was."

Dylan grinned, but there was warning in it, too. "So now you think you are old enough to criticize me, is that it?"

Trystan didn't answer; he simply stared straight ahead.

"Listen, Sir Trystan DeLanyea, new-made knight, son of a Welsh bastard."

He ignored the flush of anger spreading on the young man's cheeks. "I'm still older than you, and stronger, and a better fighter, so watch that tongue of yours or I'll be forced to knock you down."

Trystan turned glaring eyes onto him. "I don't doubt that you can beat me in a fight, but that doesn't mean I'm going to admire everything else you do."

Dylan fought a surge of temper. "What's this? A young pup dares to growl at a dog?"

"A young pup who knows when something is honorable, and when it is not."

Dylan shoved back his chair and glared at Trystan. "What are you accusing me of? How have I been dishonorable?"

Trystan got to his feet, and Dylan realized there was no fear in his eyes. "I know what is right, and what is wrong, and your marriage to Genevieve Perronet is wrong."

Dylan put his hand on his sword. "Who do you think you are to say such a thing to me?" he demanded, his words ringing out in the now-silent hall.

Suddenly aware of the silence, Dylan glanced around to see the startled faces of his foster father's friends, and to realize that the musicians had stopped in midtune.

The baron hurried toward them. "What is the trouble here?"

"Your *little boy* has the gall to tell me that he doesn't approve of my marriage."

"I'm not a child!" Trystan retorted just as angrily.

"Trystan!" the baron said sternly. "It is not for you to give approval or not. He did not have to seek it before, and he does not need it now."

He came forward and clapped a fatherly hand on his youngest son's shoulder. "Think how you would have felt if Dylan had complained of your knighthood after it was done. The marriage is made and now is a time of celebration, so you will beg his pardon. Then I will have no more such talk."

Trystan shook off the baron's hand and looked about to refuse, until he caught his father's stern eye.

He took a deep breath. "I apologize for saying such things on your wedding day," he muttered, staring at the ground.

It was obvious to Dylan that Trystan didn't think he had done wrong, any more than Dylan would if he knocked Trystan to the ground right now, as he was very tempted to do.

However, continuing this almost-sibling dispute would not sit well with the baron, whom Dylan greatly admired and loved like a father. Better to wait, and have it out with Trystan another day, he thought, if Trystan was foolish enough to repeat his charge.

Therefore, Dylan forced a magnanimous smile onto his face. "Since it is my wedding day, I am disposed to be forgiving."

A collective sigh of relief went through the hall, and the musicians again struck up a tune. The baron smiled, but the tension remained in his shoulders.

"Besides," the baron said in a jovial, if slightly strained, tone, "is it not time for the bridegroom to retire?"

Suddenly Trystan's opinion of his marriage seemed to matter very little. Instead, Dylan's thoughts flew to the bridal chamber, where beautiful Genevieve awaited him.

"You must all wish me good-night, then," he cried to the assembly.

Then he gave Trystan a sardonic glance. "Although I'm sure it will be very good whether you wish it or not."

With that, he sauntered toward the far door, laughingly accepting the good wishes, congratulations, cheers and offers of lewd advice from the baron's guests.

The baron turned to his youngest son with a condemning expression. "God's wounds, Trystan!" he growled with displeasure. "What were you thinking?"

Trystan's frown matched his father's. "He doesn't deserve her."

A look of comprehension grew in the baron's eye, yet when he spoke, his voice was stern and unyielding. "She is Dylan's wife, and there is nothing you can do to change that. You do not have to like it, but you must accept it. Do you understand me, my son?"

"I understand you, Father."

Chapter Five

Distinctly disgruntled, Dylan raised himself on his elbow to regard his sleeping wife.

She looked pretty and innocent as she slumbered, with her soft blond curls framing her delicate face. Her dusky lashes fanned upon her cheeks, and her mouth was half parted as if an invitation to a kiss.

However, her soft snores were clearly audible, and the odor of her breath enough to make him gag.

He fell back on his bed, not worried that he would wake her. He had found the empty carafe last night after getting no response from her, and it didn't take a brilliant scholar to realize she was drunk.

To think that he, Dylan DeLanyea, had found

his bride passed out on the nuptial bed on their wedding night. What sport his friends would make of this!

If they found out.

Whatever he had to do to disguise his wife's state when she awoke, he would do, rather than be the brunt of any attempted humor.

With a sour expression, he rose and stretched, reflecting that no one would have imagined he would sleep fully clothed on his wedding night, either. He went to the ewer, poured some water and then splashed his face.

Feeling somewhat refreshed, he turned and leaned back against the table, pensively regarding Genevieve.

No matter how she felt, he told himself, they would leave for Beaufort today. He had responsibilities and duties there that could not wait for her to recover.

She sighed and shifted, reminding him of the shapely body beneath the coverings, the body he had noted last night as he had tucked the sheets around her. Her breasts were perfect, her waist trim, her hips slender and her buttocks delightfully rounded.

In fact, he had actually been tempted to take her while she slept—but he was not so selfish. He could wait a little to enjoy her. After all, they were married now.

Genevieve moaned, a sound that turned into a low groan. He half smiled, recognizing that sound. She was waking, and simultaneously discovering that drinking too much wine was not a wise thing.

She rolled onto her back, then shielded her eyes with her forearm.

"Good morning, Genevieve," Dylan said, deciding he would spare her any recriminations—for the moment. She would be miserable enough, to judge by that groan.

"Dylan?"

"Yes."

"I...I am ill."

He went to the bed and regarded her with a sympathetic smile. "No, you are suffering from too much of the baron's excellent wine."

"No," she whispered, trying to sit up. "I am not well. I am going...going to be..."

Quickly Dylan grabbed the basin, threw the water onto the floor, ran to the bed and held it under Genevieve's chin. When she was finished, he set it down and fetched a cloth that he wet with cool water from the ewer. Then he gently wiped her very pale face.

She regarded him with extremely bloodshot eyes. "I'm sorry," she murmured.

"Such a result is not unexpected after too much wine, either," he remarked wryly.

She lay back on the pillow, looking so miserable, he had to pity her.

He picked up the basin. "I shall make a swift trip to the garderobe and be back quickly."

Genevieve nodded feebly.

He completed his task speedily, and when he returned, he wondered if she had fallen back to sleep, for her eyes were closed. He moved quietly toward the door so he wouldn't disturb her.

Perhaps they could wait and leave after the noon.

"Dylan?"

He turned around as she opened her bleary eyes. "Yes?"

"Send for a priest. I am dying."

"I don't think so," he replied calmly, stifling the urge to grin. She truly did look miserable—some small recompense for robbing him of his wedding night.

Thankfully there would be other nights to come.

"My head throbs, and my mouth is so dry," she said weakly. "I fear it is the plague."

"It is only a surfeit of wine, Genevieve," he said kindly. "You will be well later on."

She frowned. "I will?"

"Yes. And we must go home."

"Home?" she asked stupidly, raising her hand to her brow.

"Beaufort. It is not very far, over an easy road."

She slowly shook her head. "I cannot."

"I will get you something to ease your head, and something to eat."

"I could not eat."

He smiled affectionately. "You must. And then I shall find the gentlest mare in the baron's stable for you to ride."

"Tomorrow," she murmured, and yet with surprising resolve in her weak voice.

"No," he replied, a similar resolve in his own. "I cannot be away from my estate for much longer. It is nearly time to gather the sheep for the lambing."

"If you move me, I will surely perish."

"Unfortunately, that is a risk I will have to take."

Her head pounding as if being trampled by a herd of horses and her stomach upset, Genevieve opened her eyes to see Dylan striding out the door.

He closed it behind him with a bang that made her wince.

Very slowly and carefully she raised herself to a sitting position. By the saints, she had not felt this ill in years, if ever, and while Dylan had seemed to have a certain sympathy, he most cruelly refused to stay at Craig Fawr.

Her gaze roved over the rumpled bedclothes.

She was in her shift. He had been dressed in his black tunic, breeches and boots. She had slept the sleep of the dead. And he had slept…here?

She could not be sure. She could remember nothing after the wine.

With cautious movements, dreading what she might see, she slowly lifted the top coverings and surveyed the sheet below.

No blood.

She moved her legs. No soreness or stiffness or anything else that would indicate he had loved her.

She carefully lifted her shift and surveyed the area around her navel. Nothing there, either.

She had feared he would have even if she had been insensible. If he had not, perhaps he was not the dishonorable, lustful scoundrel she thought.

Or perhaps, she mused as she drowsily snuggled beneath the thick covers, he had imbibed too much wine, too.

* * *

Wakened again by a clattering sound and thinking Dylan must have returned, Genevieve opened one eye.

Instead of her husband, however, she saw three serving women. One carried a basin of steaming water, another fresh linen and the third seemed to have no reason beyond curiosity for being there.

Not wanting to give any cause for gossip, Genevieve kept her eyes half-closed as she watched them. Mercifully, they kept silent.

It occurred to her that when she went to Beaufort, the servants would not speak her language. How would they understand her orders and directions? She shut her eyes and stifled the urge to groan again.

"My lady?"

She squinted at the woman now bending over her who had spoken very passable French. Concern clouded her middle-aged features. "Yes?"

"The Baron DeLanyea has asked us to help you prepare for your journey."

Genevieve sighed. If the baron thought they must leave, they had little choice.

"Some bread will be brought shortly, and cold water. Would you care to wash?"

Genevieve shifted and put her feet on the floor.

Even that simple movement seemed to take too much of her vitality.

"He says you're not feeling very well. Tired, no doubt."

The serving woman glanced over her shoulder as the other women giggled. "And why not, with him the handsomest thing twixt here and London? And difficult to walk, is it?"

Genevieve gave them a disgruntled look.

"Meaning that as a compliment, my lady, for you and young Baron DeLanyea."

Genevieve blinked. Young *Baron* DeLanyea?

"My husband is a baron?"

The woman chuckled. "Yes, although he doesn't like to use the title. He says he doesn't want to sound as old as his uncle."

This news came as a welcome surprise, Genevieve thought as she slowly climbed out of the bed.

She realized her stomach felt a little better, but her mouth was still dry and her head still pounded.

Then she realized that the women were giving her rather an odd look. Perhaps she should not have revealed her ignorance of her husband's title.

"We did not speak of titles when we were together," she explained.

That made them smile again, and she felt some relief—although as she made her preparations to leave Craig Fawr, she could not help wondering what else she did not know about the man to whom she was married.

Glancing up at the cloudless sky, pleased that the day promised to be fair, Dylan sauntered toward the stables. He had given orders for his horse and one of the baron's mares to be made ready for their journey.

His uncle had given him the loan of the horse without hesitation and had also offered an additional mule for Genevieve's baggage. That was most welcome, given the size of the chest Dylan had seen in his bedchamber last night. His poor mule would have collapsed if it had had to carry both his belongings and those of his wife.

Who was not yet fully his wife.

Despite that frustrating thought, Dylan strode jauntily through the courtyard, very aware that every man present was watching him, from the lowliest groom to grim, gray-eyed Griffydd, who was only pretending to fuss with the saddle on his horse.

His guard of ten men were all assembled, ready to ride out. Judging by their disheveled appearance, Genevieve was not the only person in Craig Fawr to overimbibe the previous night.

With some relief, Dylan noted that Trystan was nowhere in sight, and he told himself it was only because he had enough to think about without worrying about Trystan's youthful opinion on a matter of which he was ignorant.

"Broken cinch, is it?" Dylan inquired as he drew near Griffydd.

"I thought it might be," Griffydd replied gravely.

Dylan smirked and Griffydd frowned.

"How is your wife?" Dylan asked.

Griffydd's expression didn't appear to change. "Better, she says."

Dylan knew that for all his inscrutability, Griffydd loved his wife passionately and was very worried about her.

Griffydd abandoned all pretext of examining his saddle. "Are you still planning on leaving today?"

"Why not?"

"That's why not," he said, nodding toward the hall behind Dylan. "Is she ill?"

Dylan glanced over his shoulder to see Genevieve slowly exit the large building, her hand clutching her uncle's arm. She looked a little green about the gills, but she was the most lovely ill-looking woman Dylan had ever seen.

He hoped the journey would not be too hard for

her and that they could reach Beaufort before nightfall. Nevertheless, the thought of spending the night under the stars with her did have a certain appeal. He glanced up at the clear blue sky. To be sure, it was a little chilly, for it was only the beginning of March, but sleeping outside would not be unbearable if they huddled together.

Behind her came serving women bearing her baggage, and he was even more glad for the additional mule. That chest in the bedchamber had, it seemed, been only one of her pieces of baggage. The three women also carried two smaller wooden boxes and a large leather pouch.

He noted that Lord Perronet's belt was weighed down by a purse whose jingling reached him even here.

Anwyl, it was a good thing Beaufort was close by, or they would be a target for every thief within fifty miles.

Despite that less than cheerful thought, he kept a smile on his face as he replied to his foster brother. ''She's just a little the worse for wine, that's all. We made very merry last night.''

Griffydd didn't reply, and Dylan thought he saw a flash of skepticism in the man's face.

It was just as well they were not staying here

any longer, he reflected as he went to meet Genevieve and her uncle.

"Good day, my lord," Dylan said jovially as he halted in front of Lord Perronet. "Just coming to see if the horses and mules were ready."

"Aren't they?" Lord Perronet demanded, peering past him toward the stable.

"They are," Griffydd called behind him.

Dylan looked over his shoulder and saw the stable door open. A groom and a stable boy led out the beasts, saddled and ready. All that remained was for Genevieve's baggage to be loaded on the mule.

Dylan gave the order, then turned to regard his bride.

"I hope you are feeling a little more rested," he said, mindful that they had an audience. Griffydd would not gossip, but he could not say the same of the servants.

A simple, quiet "Yes" was all the answer she made as she let go of her uncle's arm. She seemed to waver a bit, and he moved to help her, but she drew back a little, as if she didn't want him to touch her.

He tried not to let that trouble him.

But it did.

"Here is the dowry," Lord Perronet said abruptly.

With an expression of distaste, he pulled the purse from his belt and held it out to Dylan.

Dylan made his most charming smile as he accepted the purse, and bowed. "I thank you, my lord."

Lord Perronet nodded once.

"Take care of her, DeLanyea," he said gruffly.

"I will, my lord."

The Norman nodded once more, then turned to his niece. His expression seemed to soften for the briefest of moments. "Farewell, Genevieve. I wish you joy."

That momentary look of compassion might have been nothing more than a facial tic, for Lord Perronet's words sounded as if he expected them to have no joy at all for the rest of their lives.

"We shall be very joyful, my lord," Dylan said. "Every day and—" he let his voice drop "—every night."

That made Genevieve look at him, and while her visage expressed nothing so much as displeasure, he was satisfied with having made her look at him—and also by her uncle's shocked face.

"You have no sense of decorum, do you?" Perronet demanded.

"Very little, I'm afraid," Dylan replied lightly. "Now if you will excuse me, I will get the mule loaded, and then we can be on our way."

Genevieve watched as Dylan didn't direct the servants, but actually took some of her baggage and tied it to the mule himself.

As she did so, she tried to ignore the intense and inscrutable gaze of Griffydd DeLanyea, as well as the scrutiny of all the people in the courtyard.

She would be glad to leave this place, away from everyone who knew what she had done—unless word of her shame traveled to Dylan's home before she did.

That was a most distracting thought as her uncle gave her a cool kiss on her cheek. "Take care, Genevieve."

"Uncle, I'm sorry for all the trouble I've caused you," she whispered. "God bless you."

He nodded brusquely, turned on his heel and strode away.

Leaving her alone with all these foreign strangers.

"So, going already, is it?" a male voice inquired from somewhere close by.

The baron strode toward the stable.

Although they were leaving, Genevieve felt

comforted by his presence. Indeed, she suddenly realized she would be sorrier to leave Baron DeLanyea and his wife than her own uncle.

Even if the baron was currently regarding her with an expression she thought far too shrewd. If someone told her he knew exactly what had happened between herself and her husband last night and this morning, she would believe it.

"My lady wife sends her regrets that she cannot be here to bid you farewell, too, but my old nurse is very ill today."

"I hope she will soon be better."

The baron shook his head, a sorrowful smile on his scarred face. "Alas, she is very old. I doubt that she will live through the summer."

That shrewd look returned. "You do not look so well yourself this morning."

"I am...tired, my lord," she lied.

She had already done enough of a scandalous nature while at Craig Fawr. She would not humiliate herself further by an admission of drunkenness.

"Ah, indeed?"

His grin made her smile in response, and his eye brightened.

Dylan approached and greeted the baron.

"Glad I am that all that...practice...has not

gone to waste, boy,'' the baron said. ''Let the poor girl have some rest tonight, eh?''

''I'm not making any promises,'' Dylan replied in a seductive voice and giving her a look that made her already weak knees threaten to buckle. ''Now I think we had best be on our way, Uncle. We will take our time riding to Beaufort.''

He even said the last in that seductive tone, as if he had plans for the journey that included...what they had not done last night.

Genevieve began to fear that her face would be beet-red as long as she lived. It was enough that her head still hurt as if demons were jabbing her from within, and her empty stomach felt as if it would never be normal again. Must she be so embarrassed, too?

''Come, then, Genevieve,'' Dylan said, holding out his arm.

She placed her hand upon it and tried to ignore the hard muscles beneath her fingers as she regarded the baron and Griffydd, who came to stand beside his father. ''Goodbye, and God bless you. Give my thanks to Lady Roanna.''

''Godspeed, my dear,'' the baron said kindly.

''Godspeed,'' Griffydd repeated in a grimmer tone.

''*Anwyl*, looking morbid, you!'' Dylan chided,

giving his cousin a disdainful look before he led Genevieve to her mount. "We're only off for home."

"Aye, I know," Griffydd muttered.

Chapter Six

"Here will be a good place to rest and refresh ourselves," Dylan remarked, twisting in his saddle to regard Genevieve.

Raising her drowsy head, for she had been more than half-asleep, she saw that they had come to a bridge built over a small, gurgling stream in a wooded valley. Looking up through the trees, she guessed it was midafternoon. She could hear the water splashing over rocks, rushing away to some unknown river.

Otherwise, it was very quiet.

"Where is the escort?" she asked, realizing they were alone.

"I sent them on ahead."

"Perhaps it is not safe to stop."

He chuckled softly. "Safe as it can ever be, my lady. They were more for show, anyway."

He sounded so confident, she didn't disagree and now that she was fully awake, she wanted very much to get off the horse. Although the mare's gait was easy and smooth, the motion was not helping her stomach. Fortunately, and perhaps because of the fresh air, her head seemed much better.

Dylan swiftly dismounted and before she had moved, was beside her, ready to help her down.

She did not refuse his offer. She placed her hands on his broad shoulders, he put his on her waist, and then she slipped slowly to the ground.

Her body still close to his, he made no move to remove his hands. Neither did she as she looked up into his darkly handsome face.

For a moment, she thought he was going to kiss her—until she realized he was looking at her as a doctor would a patient.

He reached up and brushed back a stray curl from her forehead. "Feeling better?"

He sounded as dispassionate as a doctor examining a patient, too. "A little."

"Good. Have you had anything to eat today?"

"No," she confessed, reminding herself that they were, in fact and despite their marriage, little more than strangers.

"I thought not. I've brought some food from

Craig Fawr. The baron's new cook is quite a marvel with bread.''

He went to the mule tied to his horse, which held his baggage, and started to rummage in a large leather bag. "First, you need something to sit on, or the damp will ruin that gown."

Genevieve glanced down self-consciously. She had worn one of her finer dresses, for she wanted to make a good impression. On her husband's people.

Not on him, particularly.

"Here you are," he cried triumphantly, pulling out a cloak.

"Shouldn't you be wearing that?" she asked dubiously, for although the sun was shining, it was cool in the valley and a chill breeze ruffled the bare branches of the trees as well as his long hair.

"I'm not cold," he replied matter-of-factly. "Used to the weather here." He gave her a sidelong glance as he spread the dark wool garment on the grass near the stream. "Never traveled far from Wales, me."

"You have never been to London?"

His back to her, he busily adjusted the cloak. "No."

"Oh."

She envisioned Dylan in that city, among the

king's men. A man so obviously a warrior would be welcome there.

"Here you are, my lady," he said, straightening. "Sit down, and I'll fetch some bread and wine."

As he returned to the mule, he gave her a wry smile. "In your case, I think water might be better. I've got a cup here somewhere."

He began to rummage again, his head disappearing into the bag.

"I should sit on your cloak?"

"You won't hurt that," he replied, his voice muffled. "Made of good Welsh wool, that is."

"Very well."

Gingerly, because she didn't want to damage the garment despite his words, she obeyed.

"Aha!" he cried triumphantly.

Grinning, he held up a loaf and a cup, pulling his head from the bag as a conjurer would pull a coin from behind her ear. He looked so pleased, and his hair was so disheveled, she had to smile.

He came closer, his eyes sparkling with merriment as he put the loaf beside her. "Ah, better is that, to see you smile. I trust your head does not ache so badly, and your stomach is settling? I suppose you are dying of thirst?"

She nodded. "How did you know?"

"Been in your state myself more than once," he

replied with a chuckle as, swinging the cup, he walked toward the stream.

He had a very interesting walk, she decided. Athletic and virile, yet graceful, too, as if his knees were not made of bone and sinew, but something softer.

He squatted on the bank and leaned forward to fill the cup.

And then she realized his feet were sliding on the wet grass, toward the water.

"Dylan!" she cried, jumping up.

He heard her warning, dropped the cup and tried to stand.

Too late.

With a bellow like an enraged bull, he lost his balance and fell into the stream.

She ran forward, envisioning his death by drowning as he flailed in the water. Then she saw that he was only trying to maintain his balance in the rocky stream, his efforts accompanied by what she suspected were Welsh profanities.

"Here," she said, holding out her hand. "Let me help you."

His clothing soaking, his hair sodden, he gave her a sullen look as he continued to teeter, waving his arms like some kind of strange bird attempting to fly.

"Take my hand!"

Cautiously, he did so, his long fingers wrapping around hers. She pulled—and then felt her own feet sliding out from under her. "No! Stop!"

In the next instant, she, too, was in the frigid stream. Fortunately, she was not completely immersed, for he pulled her close and held her up. Nevertheless, her feet and legs and the bottom of her gown were in the incredibly cold water.

He looked at her, a different sort of smile on his handsome face, and she became very aware of the sensation of his strong arms around her.

And that she must look like an imbecile, as well as completely undignified. Then, to add to her embarrassment, her teeth started to chatter.

"We had better dry off," he said softly, "and get you warm. How will it look if you fall ill after only one day in my care?"

Too cold to speak, she could only nod, until he picked her up. "Don't!" she cried as he took a tentative step forward. "Put me down!"

"I won't drop you, my lady," he assured her— just as a rock beneath his foot shifted. He held her out like some kind of offering to the gods for a brief moment, and then they both fell into the rushing water.

Spluttering, Genevieve struggled to her feet, her

wet gown and cloak a sodden, spoiled mass of heavy fabric, her cap and veil bedraggled.

"I told you to put me down!" she cried angrily, regarding her equally wet, sodden companion.

"I was only trying to be chivalrous," he replied, likewise staggering to his feet. "I didn't want you to get completely wet."

"Well, my lord, obviously you failed!"

His lips twitched as if he was trying not to laugh. "I suppose one could say that."

With a disdainful sniff that came out sounding more like a snivel, she grabbed her skirt and started to make her way to the bank.

"Careful!" he cautioned behind her.

She gave him a scornful look over her shoulder as she neared the bank. "I suggest you follow your own advice."

"I will try," he replied gravely.

On her hands and knees, she started to crawl out of the stream. Finally reaching his cloak, she sat, shivering, and stared at her completely ruined, grass-stained gown.

She looked up when Dylan sat beside her. He lifted the ends of his cloak and wrapped them about her as a mother would tuck in an infant at night. "I will build a fire."

"Please do."

"In the meantime, you must take off those wet clothes."

"Where?"

"Where what?" he asked as he rose.

"Where can I take them off?"

"Anywhere. There's no one nearby."

She stared at him in disbelief. "In the open? I will certainly get a chill that way."

He gave her a wry grin. "I think modesty a very attractive quality in a woman."

It suddenly struck her that he didn't even have goose bumps, while she felt chilled to the marrow of her bones. "And I think vanity is a deplorable attribute in a man."

He apparently lost the inclination to consider her state at all funny.

"Have you another cloak?" he asked.

"Yes, my winter one. It is in the large chest."

He nodded and went to the mule behind her horse. She couldn't see what he was doing, but she could imagine him foraging through her belongings with no care at all for the careful packing of the maidservants.

"I hope you're not making a mess of everything," she complained quietly, but loud enough for him to hear.

"Would you rather wait?"

Since she had never felt so cold in her life, she didn't make any answer.

He pulled forth her fur-lined cloak, the same one she had worn in the garden. If he recalled the last time he had seen it—the time he had made her believe that he loved her—he made no sign. Instead, he went to the bare, low-lying branches of an oak and threw the top of the cloak over it, so that the rest of the garment hung down like a drapery. "There, my lady. You may have your modesty behind that."

Holding his cloak, which smelled of horse and leather and *him,* she got to her feet. "Did you see the dark green gown? The one with the gold embroidery? I would wear that. And a shift and stockings, of course. And I will require my brush."

His eyes narrowed ever so slightly. "Anything else, my lady? Perhaps some mulled wine and a pheasant stew?"

She lifted her chin as she turned to walk toward the oak tree. "While I would appreciate both, I shall settle for the dry clothing and my brush."

Dylan scowled as he went back to the chest to find what she requested. She was addressing him as if he were nothing more than her servant. *Anwyl,* he was her husband, and freezing to boot. She seemed to have forgotten that he had fallen into the stream first, and been in the cold water longer. Nor did she give him thanks for indulging her request for a private place to change when he would have been better employed building a fire.

And she had his one and only cloak, which was surely now soaking wet, when he might want it to warm himself after he had gotten into dry clothes. Did any grateful thought of that enter her pretty Norman head? Apparently not.

Muttering an oath, he found the dress. It was a very fine dress, considering they were traveling and she needed something warm. This green gown was thin and more appropriate for a feast in a warm hall than riding in the chill of a spring afternoon. He lifted out another one or two, and finally found something more suitable, a heavy dark brown wool dress, plain and unembellished. He discovered a shift and then some appropriately thick stockings. He also retrieved a pair of boots from his own baggage, for all her footwear seemed decidedly flimsy.

He turned around—and muttered another oath, for he caught a brief glimpse of her bare leg. Her long, slender bare leg, the sight of which arousingly reminded him that he had not yet made love with his wife.

He shivered—from the cold, of course—and strode toward the makeshift drapery.

"Here are some dry clothes," he announced, reaching around the cloak, the bundle in his outstretched hand.

She made no move to take the clothing. "I cannot wear that! And where did those horrible boots come from? Someone must have put them in my baggage by mistake."

"It was the warmest dress I could find, and the boots belong to me. You need something more than flimsy slippers."

"They'll fall right off my feet. I need the green dress—and I do not see my brush!"

"That gown is too fine and too thin. You'll get sick."

"I want the green one!" she repeated petulantly.

Truly frustrated, he threw the bundle of clothing on the ground, grabbed the cloak and yanked it from the branch.

"What are you doing?" she shrieked.

She was not naked, or rather, not completely, for she was wrapped in his damp cloak.

"I will tell you what I am *not* doing," he said as he tried to ignore the sight of her bare shoulders and angry face. "I am not fetching you another gown as if I were your serving wench. I have chosen something warm and serviceable, and that is what you will wear. You will put on my boots without another word of complaint. If you want your hairbrush, you can get it yourself. Now I am going to get into my own dry clothes and then we will be on our way.''

She flushed, still defiant. ''You were going to build a fire.''

''I've changed my mind. We will finish our journey instead.'' With that, he spun on his heel and marched to the mule carrying his baggage.

Then he started to strip off his wet clothes, not caring if Genevieve watched or not.

She did not. Instead, she put on her dry shift, stockings and his large boots before she froze to death. She picked up the ugly brown dress, uttered a small sigh of resignation and pulled it on.

Dylan had been too angry for her to risk further displeasure. After all, she was totally at her husband's mercy in the wilds of Wales.

Finished, she put on her warm fur-lined cloak and picked up his damp one, finally looking at him.

He was dressed in different clothing, although the new tunic and breeches were also black. At the moment, he was bent over, tugging on his boots, and his still-wet hair curled about his red face.

Comfortably warm now, she approached him warily. He straightened and regarded her with a gaze as cold as the waters of the stream.

"I see you have some sense, after all," he said.

She held out his cloak and he snatched it from her, throwing it over the back of his horse.

"Where is the bread?" she asked, trying to act as if nothing untoward had happened.

"*Anwyl!*" he muttered angrily, moving away from her and surveying the area where the cloak had been spread. "Didn't you take it?"

"No."

"There it is."

He went a few paces and picked up the loaf, now dotted with dirt. He started to brush it off.

"We cannot eat that."

"I can. If you would rather not, then don't."

"I would rather not."

"Then don't."

"I won't!" she declared as he bit into the bread and ripped off a great chunk with his teeth.

She walked toward the stream.

"What are you doing?" he demanded, his mouth still full of bread.

"Finding your cup."

"Don't fall."

"I'll try not to," she said through clenched

teeth, keeping well back from the slippery bank.
"I cannot see it."

"Probably far downstream by now. I'll ask my
shepherds who take care of this portion of my land
to keep an eye out for it."

She turned to him. "This is your land?"

"From the first fork in the road from Craig Fawr
we have been on my land."

"Oh."

He was already finished the bread and, brushing
the crumbs from his hands, he strolled toward her.
"I am a baron, you see."

"So I was told."

His brow furrowed ominously. "Who told you
that?"

"The serving women at Craig Fawr."

"What else did they tell you?"

"Nothing. Since I can't understand Welsh, I
have no idea what else they said. However, I gather
I am to be delighted you are my husband."

He grinned. "Naturally."

When he looked like that, she found it hard to
meet his gaze. "Dylan, I..." She took a deep
breath. "I am sorry this happened."

"I've slipped and fallen before this."

She raised her eyes and this time, found the

strength not to look away. "No, I meant the marriage."

His grin disappeared, replaced by a grim frown. "It is not how I thought such a thing would happen," he said in a voice just as grim as his expression. "But what is done, is done. I am willing to make the best of it, if you are."

She nodded.

He smiled again, with something like his usual bonhomie. After all, there could be worse brides than Genevieve Perronet, even if she was evincing more stubbornness than he would have suspected. "Good. Now let us mount and go on to Beaufort. It is not far now."

She looked down at her dress, that petulant frown on her face again. He thought she mumbled something.

"What is it?"

She made a mournful face. "I still want to wear my green gown."

Before he could say anything, she rushed on. "I want to make a good impression when I get to your home. I look like a peasant in this...this *sack*."

"Why didn't you say so when I first brought it to you?"

Her hands behind her back, she looked at the ground and shrugged her slender shoulder. Even that motion was surprisingly graceful, and attractive.

"We can stop when we're nearly there and you can put the green gown on," he said. "Will that suit you?"

She raised her eyes and nodded, just once, reminding him rather uncomfortably of her uncle. Fortunately, she was much prettier.

"How are you feeling?" he asked.

Her large blue eyes widened with surprise. "Why, better."

"Nothing like time and a dunk in a stream to clear a head suffering from a surfeit of wine," he declared as he walked toward her horse.

Genevieve thought she had already had enough surprises this day; however, when they reached the top of a low hill and saw the castle beside the wide river in the valley below, she had another.

She had not expected Dylan's castle to be so large and imposing. Moreover, an obviously prosperous village stood near the castle, the houses spreading along the three roads leading to the castle like leaves on the branches of a tree. The surrounding hillsides, some parts covered with trees, others open, were dotted with sheep. In the fields, peasants were at work, already sowing grain.

"That is Beaufort," he declared proudly, if unnecessarily, speaking for the first time since they had left the bridge.

He was not looking at her. He looked at the sight before him, and there was a smile of both pride and pleasure on his face—and a rather unexpected shrewdness, as if he were taking stock of the activity.

She had not really considered him the master of an estate, and yet, as she looked at him now, she realized that was precisely what he looked like: the master of all he surveyed.

"It is most impressive, my lord," she said softly, and truthfully.

He turned to her with a pleased, infectious grin. "It is, isn't it?" Then he sighed. "Not as impressive as it could be, but give me time."

She had not thought him an ambitious man, either.

"When we get to that little wood near the village, you can put on your green dress and impress everybody."

She nodded, pleased that he had remembered.

"Ah! Now they have seen us," he announced cheerfully as he raised his hand in greeting.

She followed his gaze and realized that there did

seem to be some bustle behind the merlons on the castle walls.

Dylan nudged his horse to a walk, and she followed suit. Together they made their way along the well-kept road, until he pulled his mount to a stop just inside the wood, which was very small. It was also very sparse since the trees were not in leaf.

"I...I cannot change my clothing here."

He looked around. "This is the last place before any of my people's lodgings. I think you look lovely as you are, but if you want to put on the other dress, it will have to be here."

She flushed at his compliment, but it could not subvert the anxiety that had taken hold of her at the thought of her arrival at Beaufort as the unexpected, unknown wife of the lord. "I shall put on the dress."

Dylan dismounted and came to help her but she had already gotten off the mare by herself.

"I hope it is not too wrinkled," she said, biting her lip as she went toward the mule.

"I am no lady's maid to be packing gowns."

He spoke as if her uneasiness were only a childish indulgence.

With swift, annoyed motions, she tried to undo

the knot in the rope holding the baggage to the mule.

"There is no need for that," Dylan said behind her.

He stepped in front of her and, in a few deft movements, had the lid open, for the chest was bound to the mule not by the rope encircling it but by bindings tied through the leather handles at the sides. "And here is the green gown right on the top."

He pulled it out, and she noted with relief that it wasn't any more wrinkled than it would have been if packed away by an expert.

"I would suggest behind that bush, my lady."

She glanced over her shoulder where he had gestured with his head and saw a thick holly bush. "Very well."

He held out the gown, but when she went to take it, he didn't let go right away. "It takes more than a gown to make a lady."

"But a fine gown helps," she retorted as she marched toward the holly bush.

She wanted everyone in Beaufort to know she came from a fine and wealthy family. She had not spend eight long years with Lady Katherine learning to be the chatelaine of a castle only to look like a poor pilgrim when she first entered her husband's home.

She wanted everyone to respect her, too.

She knew her looks were against her in that regard, with her blond curls, blue eyes and rosy complexion. For a long time at Lady Katherine's, all the other girls had treated her as a sort of pet, and at first that had been more than acceptable, for it meant they indulged and spoiled her. Even the strict and stern Lady Katherine seemed to loosen some of her rules for Genevieve.

Yet as she had grown into womanhood, it had dawned on her that to be spoiled and petted was to be treated as a sort of perpetual child, incapable of adult decisions.

Perhaps, she reflected as she made her way behind the sharply pointed, dark green leaves, she had even believed that a little herself, or she might have found the strength to protest her betrothal instead of resorting to the method she had chosen.

She removed the detested brown dress and threw it over the bush. It crossed her mind to leave it there as she drew on the lovely green gown, but that would not be practical.

She adjusted the bodice of her gown, and stretched, trying to tie the laces. They were not within easy reach, and as she twisted and turned like an eel in a sack, she suddenly heard a series of yells and shrill shrieks.

Childish yells and girlish shrieks, she realized even as she shoved her way through the thorny holly—to see Dylan wrestling with two ragged urchins apparently intent on pummeling him into submission, while a little girl about five years old jumped up and down, and clapped her hands with glee.

"Stop! Stop this!" Genevieve cried.

Other young ladies left to the tender care of Lady Katherine would have recognized the tone Genevieve unconsciously mimicked, and likewise halted.

The boys, who looked about ten and eight years old, and a disheveled Dylan, straightened. Her lordly husband had a sheepish grin on his face, and his eyes twinkled with unsuppressed merriment.

Both dark-haired boys would have been good-looking if they had been clean, Genevieve thought as they regarded her gravely, their gazes uncomfortably suspicious and intense. The little girl, whose hair was a rather shockingly bright red, stuck a finger in her mouth and stared at her with undisguised curiosity.

"What is going on here?" she demanded, wondering how these ragamuffins could have the gall to behave in this bizarre manner unless they were not quite right in the head.

Dylan laid a hand on the older, brown-eyed boy's shoulder. "This is Trefor."

He put his other hand on the gray-eyed lad's head. "This is Arthur."

He smiled at the girl. "And that little darling is Gwethalyn."

He looked at Genevieve. "These are my children."

Chapter Seven

Dylan's hand gripped Trefor's shoulder so hard, his son twisted away.

It was not that Dylan was ashamed of his children—not at all—but he had hoped to tell Genevieve about them in his own way.

Indeed, he had meant to do it on the journey to Beaufort, but she had not been feeling well. Then they had fallen into the stream and she had been annoyed—hardly the frame of mind he wanted this highborn Norman lady to be in when he told her that he was credited with three children born out of wedlock, by three different women.

Then he had thought to do so when they neared the castle. Unfortunately, he had not expected the children to be lying in wait to meet him, especially this late in the day.

This late in the day. He looked at Trefor, and away from Genevieve's startled face. "How is it your mother lets you run about the woods with the sun setting, eh? And Arthur and Gwethalyn's mothers, too. Do none of them have a care what could have happened if I was late or had decided to stay an extra day at Craig Fawr? You would have been benighted in the woods!"

"Mothers?" Genevieve asked weakly, with a slight emphasis on the plural.

Dylan bit back a curse. He should have spoken Welsh.

"Who is she?" Gwethalyn demanded in lisping Welsh, not for a moment taking her steadfast gaze from Genevieve, or at least Genevieve's clothes.

"This is Lady Genevieve," he replied, this time in their native tongue, glancing at his wife.

He noted that Genevieve was apparently so stunned, she had not realized her bodice was still undone, the neckline gaping. "My bride."

"What?" the boys cried simultaneously, and in obvious disbelief.

"I will tell you all about it when we get home."

"Mothers—more than one?" Genevieve repeated with more assertion.

"I will explain."

"I should think so."

He almost scowled at her, but at nearly the same moment, she realized that her shift was showing. She grabbed the neck of her bodice and pulled it up, a bright blush stealing over her smooth cheeks.

"I require some assistance, my lord," she said haughtily. "I cannot reach the laces."

Dylan glanced at his sons and saw that they were regarding her with a mixture of shock, dismay and curiosity.

Why not? With her blond hair, expensive gown and the additional fascination of being their father's bride, why should they not stare?

"Is she a princess?" Gwethalyn asked in an awestruck whisper.

"No, a Norman," Dylan replied as he went toward Genevieve. He stepped behind her. "You boys may ride my horse, if you like."

As he assisted her, he had to force himself to keep his mind on her laces, not the expanse of naked neck and back before him that seemed to cry out for his kiss or caress.

The boys stopped staring and ran toward his stallion. Trefor got there first, his legs being longer. He had a struggle to get onto the beast's back, however. Arthur, competitive from the cradle, kept tugging on his leg.

"Trefor, help him up behind you," Dylan ordered. "You may be in the front halfway, then he shall have a turn—and don't make that face at me, or I'll speak to your mother."

Sulking, Trefor reached down his hand and pulled Arthur into place.

Genevieve marched to her horse and got on it without waiting for his assistance, so he scooped up the little Gwethalyn and grinned at her.

"You may ride the mule," he said, putting her atop the beast, "and if you look in that little bag there, you will find something from Lady Roanna for you."

Gwethalyn's smile was like sunshine after rain. Genevieve had a lovely smile, too, but, reflected Dylan, it might be some time before he saw that again, if her manner was any indication.

"We can go in a moment," he said, hurrying to the holly bush.

He gathered up Genevieve's brown dress and her cloak. "I think you are forgetting something, my lady."

"Not as much as you have, apparently."

He strode toward her horse and, without warning, threw the garments at her. She caught them deftly, something that didn't help his mood, although he would have been equally annoyed had they landed on the ground.

Then he went to the head of her horse and grabbed the bridle.

"Lead the way, Trefor," he commanded, trying not to sound angry, for he was not annoyed with them. "Arthur, keep an eye on Gwethalyn."

He switched to Norman French. "I didn't forget my children."

"Just to tell me about them," Genevieve pointed out as she tried to keep the garments from falling to the ground. She managed to lay the gown over her knees.

She was not at all happy to have yet another reminder—and such a reminder!—of how little she knew of her husband.

"What's the matter? Don't you like children?"

"Yes, of course I do," she snapped as she tried to get the cloak over her shoulders.

"Good. I want us to have a lot of them."

She flushed hotly as she attempted, with suddenly clumsy fingers, to tie her cloak around her neck.

Then she thought of a reason he might not have mentioned the mothers of these children and wished she could call back her words. "Did their mothers…die?"

His harsh bark of a laugh startled her. "No. They are all in fine health."

He gave her a searching glance over his shoulder, then faced forward again. "I have never been married before. Trefor's mother is Angharad, a seamstress in the village. Arthur's mother is Mair, who makes ale, and Gwethalyn's mam is Llannulid. She recently married my steward."

"Then these children are all...?"

"Bastards?" he proposed with a hint of bitterness, again glancing at her over his shoulder. "Aye, like their father."

"Then I should think you, of all men, might have some reasons to avoid producing them."

He halted and faced her. "There is something you had better understand at once, my lady. In Wales, it is no sin to love a woman, and if a child is a result, no shame to mother or children, whether in wedlock or no, as long as the man doesn't abandon his responsibility toward them."

"Obviously your notion of responsibility does not include lawful marriage."

He turned back and started walking again, without answering.

She hated being ignored, as if she was not worthy of answer, yet in this instance, she took his haughty silence as evidence that he appreciated that while his behavior may not be shameful to him, or his women, or his children, she thought very differently. "Perhaps it is your intention to increase the population of your estate single-handedly."

He wheeled around and in two strides was beside her. "The children are taught your tongue, but so far they have been spared Norman arrogance, so I would watch what comes from that pretty mouth of yours. They will find out soon enough what the Normans think of bastards, as I did, but I would spare them that knowledge as long as I can."

Her gaze faltered. In truth, she had not thought of the children at all.

And in one sense he was right. It was not the children's fault their father was what he was, and that their mothers cared so little for their honor, or their own happiness. Surely they had been saddened when he left each of them for another.

What would they think of her, his wife?

"I am glad you see the error of your ways," he muttered, clearly interpreting her silence as contrition before he resumed leading her horse toward their destination.

"But do you see the error of yours?" she whispered, thinking not just of his bastard children, but of their mothers, who must have been heartbroken when their liaison with Dylan was at an end.

* * *

Their arrival in the village was cause for much boisterous shouting and greeting, both on the part of the villagers, and Dylan and his children. As for the village itself, it seemed prosperous enough, although laid out in a most random fashion, with no central green or other meeting area.

Perhaps the courtyard of the castle served this function, she reasoned.

Her dismay grew as they approached the hulking gray stone edifice that dominated the village and the river below it.

From the surrounding hill, all seemed neat and efficient; upon closer viewing, this proved to be an illusion.

As they entered, followed by a crowd of villagers and what looked like soldiers who had deserted their sentry posts, she surveyed the buildings, comparing them to her uncle's castle, and others she had seen. It appeared that Beaufort castle was at its best viewed from a distance.

The main buildings of Beaufort were excellent, in and of themselves—well-built of stone, large and strong. Additions had been made, however, of wattle-and-daub, and these seemed to be in immediate need of repair and maintenance. The area outside the stable was muddy and messy, the roof covering the well decrepit, and a haphazard pile of wood was on the ground outside what she assumed was the kitchen, exposed to the elements.

More startling, perhaps, was the sudden appearance of what might have been every servant and hireling in the place. Did they not have duties to perform?

Dylan, however, seemed to find nothing wrong with this impromptu celebration; indeed, he called out jovial responses and looked happier than she had seen him since...since before their wedding.

Genevieve also watched the gathering crowd, and would never have admitted, even to herself, that her gaze sought out women who looked of an age to be the mothers of Dylan's children.

Nearly at the stables, Dylan tossed her mare's rein to a waiting stable boy as his sons slid from the back of his horse. It was clear they were enjoying immensely all the attention they were receiving.

Genevieve waited expectantly for Dylan to assist her.

He lifted Gwethalyn from the mule instead. She immediately ran to a pretty young woman with raven hair and dark brown eyes, a woman who hugged her close and smiled at Dylan.

That must be the girl's mother with the outlandish, unpronounceable name, Genevieve decided.

She wondered if the boys would also go to their respective mothers, but before she could see where they went, Dylan came to stand beside her mare.

"Shall I assist you, my lady?" he asked politely.

She nodded regally and allowed him to do so. Surrounded by the curious crowd, she found it easier to ignore the sensation of his hands on her waist, especially since she was determined to act with all the dignity she could muster.

Dylan smiled at her, but she saw the searching look in his eyes before he took her hand and turned to address the people.

She had no idea what he said, except for her name, but it was easy to guess by the startled looks on their faces. He had announced he had brought home a wife.

She tried to betray nothing. To look composed. To act as if she married immoral, dark-haired, seductive Welshmen every day.

Then, after what seemed an age, the crowd started to applaud and stamp their feet, shouting out "Dy-*lan!* Dy-*lan!*"

Grinning, he gave her a sidelong glance and his grip tightened around her hand.

"Smile," he admonished in a whisper. "You look like you're at a wake."

"You're hurting me," she chastised quietly through clenched teeth as she nevertheless obeyed.

His grip relaxed slightly as he turned to her, and now she could not read the expression in his dark brown eyes.

"Welcome to Beaufort, my lady."

Dylan had not expected Genevieve to be utterly delighted when she arrived at Beaufort. The highly unusual circumstances surrounding their marriage would ensure that, if nothing else.

However, did she have to look as if she would rather be anywhere else in the entire world? Or as if their reception, so pleasing to him, was cause for contempt?

He reminded himself that she did not have the reason he did to be so happy with his people's boisterous welcome; nevertheless, she had no cause to be so obviously displeased, either.

As he led her toward his hall, he surveyed his castle. To be sure, there could be some improvements, but it was a fine place, well made and nearly impregnable.

Of course, she had had a great shock when Trefor, Arthur and Gwethalyn had appeared and she had learned who they were—but then so had he, when he had awoken to find her in his bed and her irate uncle about to attack him.

Or perhaps this haughty Norman was used to being the center of attention, and begrudged him his welcome for that reason alone.

Well, she would simply have to get used to that. After all, if there was anyone who deserved to be in a bad humor, it was the man who had been tricked into marriage, not the woman who had tricked him.

And for a woman who had claimed she wanted to make a good first impression, she seemed abysmally ignorant of how to achieve that goal.

They entered his hall. Around the central hearth, the bare tables were set for the evening meal, placed with no particular regard for order. Some linen beyond the usual well-worn napkins might have been nice, but he could not fault his servants. They had had little warning, save from the escort sent on ahead, that he was bringing home a bride.

Nor would he complain that the fire seemed particularly smoky. There had been much rain of late, and perhaps no dry wood could be found.

He glanced at the one and only chair on the dais. Genevieve would have to make do with the end of a bench.

A lovely smell of roasting meat and stew drifted to him from the kitchens, and he smiled contentedly. Genevieve might think the furnishings of his hall and the table settings lacking, but she could not fault his cook.

He had no time to consider much else, for the crowd followed them inside the hall. The serving women hurried to their duties and his men went to the tables, ready for their meal.

He caught the attention of one of the women and issued a brief order before escorting Genevieve to the table on the dais.

Father Paulus shoved his way through the noisy gathering and folded his hands. The hall fell silent as he started to say the grace in Latin, which was sure to please the bride.

Genevieve stared at slender, gray-haired Father Paulus as if she had never seen a priest before.

"What is wrong now?" Dylan demanded in a whisper.

"What is he saying?"

"The grace before we eat."

"Is that Welsh?"

"No. Latin."

She gave him a skeptical, sidelong glance. "That isn't Latin. Or Greek. Or French. Or Italian, either."

"I suppose you speak all those, that you know it is not?" he asked just as skeptically.

"Yes, I do."

He continued to regard Father Paulus steadily. "He has been a long time from Rome or Canterbury."

"If he was ever there at all."

"What are you implying?"

"Nothing, my lord, except that if he claims that is Latin, he is wrong."

"You think he *lies?*"

She shrugged her shoulders and at the same moment, the grace—or whatever it was—ended, and the whole cacophonous company took their places on the benches, ready to eat.

"Father Paulus will be sitting beside me," Dylan announced somewhat defensively, obviously expecting her to object. However, that was right and proper, provided this man really was a priest.

Almost immediately, the priest was at his elbow.

"Welcome home, my lord," he said in the deepest voice Genevieve had ever heard and with a wary look at her. "Welcome to you, too, my lady."

She inclined her head in acknowledgment before she took her place on the end of the bench nearest the center of the large, scarred and unadorned table.

The priest—alleged priest, she inwardly amended—took his seat on the bench on the other side of Dylan as the first dish arrived on the table.

It was not bread. Or soup. It was a platter of roasted chicken.

The bread should come first, and the wine should already have been poured.

She glanced at Dylan, but he was deep in conversation with the priest and seemed to find nothing amiss with the serving of the meal, which continued in the same haphazard fashion. Courses arrived in no particular order, at any table, so that some things were cold by the time they reached the high table, which should always be served first.

The linen napkins were gray and stained, and hers even had an unmended tear. Later, she wondered what had happened to the wine, for after the first goblet had finally been poured, no more arrived at their table.

The meal was constantly interrupted as a bevy of men came to the table and spoke with Dylan. With pointed politeness, he introduced each one to her. Unfortunately, there were so many and their names were so odd, she could not remember them all.

In fact, there was only one man whose name she was able to recall with any ease, Thomas-y-Tenau. That was because he was the steward and, therefore, the new husband of little Gwethalyn's mother.

As for what all these men had to say, Genevieve assumed it was estate business; however, she had no way of knowing, since they spoke Welsh.

She supposed it could be worse. They could be women coming to pester him.

Several times she noted the serving wenches smiling at Dylan, and she couldn't help wondering if the three children she had met were all he had fathered. She looked for the two boys and their mothers, but didn't see anything of Trefor or Arthur.

She stopped searching the hall when Gwethalyn's mother gave her a knowing, sympathetic look, which Genevieve did not deign to acknowledge.

Genevieve concluded the meal was over when a considerable time had passed without the arrival of more food, which was, she had to admit, delicious.

Genevieve regarded her husband as he listened intently to Thomas, who had come again to speak to him. One hand on his chin, Dylan nodded thoughtfully.

Seen thus, it was easy to believe he was the commander of a castle.

She cocked her head to one side, wondering which guise she preferred: the seductive stranger or the lord of a mighty fortress?

Then she reminded herself such thoughts were a waste of time. Whatever guise he assumed, one thing remained unequivocal: he was her lawful husband, and he should not be ignoring her.

She cleared her throat. Neither of the men so much as glanced at her.

She coughed.

Still they paid no attention.

She coughed again, loudly.

No response.

Finally, she reached out and plucked at Dylan's sleeve.

Startled out of his discussion, he looked at her quizzically.

"My lord, is there no more wine?" she asked.

His lips curled up in a smile that seemed even more seductive than any she had yet seen him make.

As for the expression in his eyes...she grew so warm, she had to look away.

"You have had enough wine," he said quietly. "I will not have you sleep too soon tonight."

She swallowed hard, then stood up. "If you will excuse me, my lord, I...I think...I think I will... retire."

"By all means." Dylan gestured at one of the young serving women. "Cait will show you to our bedchamber."

Chapter Eight

Finally alone, Genevieve looked around the untidy chamber that the young woman had shown her.

The first thing to draw her attention was the large and imposing bed, with its messy coverings that looked as if they had not been touched since Dylan had last got out of it.

She blushed as she recalled Dylan, naked, leaping from the bed at Craig Fawr.

She forced her attention back to the furnishings, which included a bronze brazier, empty of coals; a candle stand with room for six candles, filled and lighted; a table for ewer and basin; a stool; and a large wooden chest. The single, tall, slender window was covered by a linen shutter. Pale moonlight illuminated the fabric.

Her baggage and some that she recognized from the back of Dylan's mule had been piled in a corner. She supposed she could have asked the woman to help her unpack it, but she hadn't known if the servant spoke anything but Welsh. Rather than have to signal her wishes, and suddenly very desirous of being alone, Genevieve had gestured for the woman to go, then closed the door after her.

Now it was time to prepare to get into that vast bed and...sleep.

Genevieve found the silken shift intended for her wedding night with Lord Kirkheathe.

Why not? This was her bridal night.

With fingers that *would* tremble, she removed her green gown and linen shift, and put on the silken garment. Its smooth softness brushed her skin in a way no clothing ever had before.

Or maybe it was anxiety that made her so aware of the feel of the fabric and the warm scent of the candle wax. She heard soft male voices below and paused a moment, trying to decipher the different timbres, seeking Dylan's.

Giving up, she searched in her baggage for the small vial of perfume, a parting gift from Lady Katherine. She almost wished she was back at Lady Katherine's with the other girls.

Almost.

She found the vial and pulled out the stopper, releasing a pleasant odor of roses.

Dylan had kissed her with unbridled desire in a rose garden.

Her hands still trembling, she put on a little of the scent, then found her hairbrush. She brushed her hair until it was free of tangles. Then she blew out all the candles save one and climbed into the bed.

If she had been waiting for Lord Kirkheathe, would she have been so nervous?

Probably, she thought.

Yet beneath her nervousness, she knew she was feeling something else, something that added to her tension.

She was excited, exhilarated by the same emotions that had made her believe she was in love with Dylan DeLanyea and must marry him.

So now she was married to him, and shortly he would come to this room. To this bed. And he would make her fully his wife.

Unless he had decided to spend the night with somebody else.

A shiver of fear combined with anger ran down her spine. Surely he wouldn't—

Her grip tightened as the door began to open.

It seemed to take forever for Dylan to come into

the room. He glanced at the bed, then closed the door softly behind him. He turned to regard her, his face half-hidden in shadows, his expression unreadable.

Finally he strolled toward the remaining candle. His eyes remained shadowed, but a smile grew on his face, a smile that made her start to tremble with anticipation—and dread. He had had so many lovers, and she none. What if he found her lacking?

At that thought, she felt tears come to her eyes and looked down at the coverings so he wouldn't see them as she struggled to regain her self-control.

"Cait told me you sent her away," he said matter-of-factly.

"Yes," she answered quietly. "I didn't require any help."

"She was afraid she had offended you."

"No," she replied, glancing at him to find him regarding her steadily.

"Sensitive is Cait, to be sure," he replied with a slightly critical tone. "But you might have said something to her. She thinks you hate her."

"I didn't think she would understand me."

"Most of the servants speak a little of the Normans' tongue. She would have understood a 'thank-you.'"

"Oh," Genevieve replied feebly.

He sauntered toward the bed. "It will be easier when you learn some Welsh."

"You think I should learn their language?"

He frowned with displeasure. "It's my language, too, and you're living in Wales now."

He was right, of course. That had simply never occurred to her.

"Very well," she said, looking away from his piercing dark eyes.

He went to the washstand. "The best person to help you at the start would be Llannulid, I should think."

"Gwethalyn's mother?"

She was not at all delighted by the prospect of relying upon her husband's former lover for anything.

He pulled off his tunic, revealing his muscular back. "Yes."

She didn't reply as he splashed cold water on his face. Besides, what was there to say? She could guess that he would not understand her feelings on this matter, given everything he had said before.

He dried his face and looked at her. "There is no need to be jealous. Our liaison was over before Gwethalyn was born."

"That you are fickle is supposed to encourage me?"

"No," he replied with unlooked-for understanding. "I meant only to reassure you."

He approached the bed, his naked chest seeming to glow in the dim light.

She held her breath as he sat beside her. He reached out and took her hand from the covers.

Could he feel her trembling? she wondered as he gently pressed a kiss upon the back of it.

He raised his eyes and regarded her gravely. "Genevieve, I will speak of these things tonight, and then I wish to be done with them. Believe me when I tell you no one could have forced me to marry you if I had been adamantly against it. My uncle would not have insisted, and your uncle's threats would have been useless.

"As for the women I have loved, that is in the past. I intend to be faithful to my wife, no matter how she came to be my wife. Do you understand?"

She regarded him steadily. "I cannot understand how you can have loved so many women."

"I did love them, or so I thought at the time, and they felt something for me. As time passed, the feelings changed. Mellowed, or altered, whatever you wish to call it, so that the women and I both knew when it was time for an end."

"You don't love me."

"That can change."

"I don't love you, either."

A slight frown darkened his features. "I thought that was why you came to my bed."

"I believed you loved me then, and I..." Her whisper trailed off into a sorrowful sigh.

His soft lips brushed her palm. "Do you think you can never love me, lovely Genevieve?"

She pulled her hand away, the better to think. "I...I don't know."

"I am not sure what I feel for you, either," he said as his lips curled up in a devilish smile. "Shall we try to find out? Wife."

He leaned forward as he tugged the coverings from her loosened grasp. Then he kissed her with all the passion he had before, and more.

As she felt the delicious sensation of his lips upon hers, thoughts of his other women slipped away. She yielded to the desire that had been growing within her ever since he had come into the room, and before, telling herself he had to care for her if he kissed her with such passion.

His hands traveled up her arms to her shoulders, drawing her closer. Then she felt him untying the lace at the neck of her shift, so that it loosened.

His tongue pushed into her mouth. She remembered this—and yet it was different, here in the night, in the bed.

There was no reason to stop now, no need to feel embarrassed or ashamed.

Except one.

She pulled away shyly. "I don't quite know what to do," she whispered.

Dylan smiled at his pretty wife, who had a face so innocent, and a response so seductive. *Anwyl*, he had never known a woman like her, or one that inflamed him so.

"It is not difficult," he replied with a throaty chuckle, moving and pulling her with him so that they were lying beside each other. "We shall go slowly, so that you can learn."

She nodded gravely, the corona of her curls around her face glowing like a halo.

He brushed one back from her forehead with his finger.

"I mean it, Genevieve," he vowed softly. "As you are my wife, I will be faithful to you. So put away your fears, and know that I am happy it is so."

"You...you are?"

"I have said it, haven't I?"

"Truly?"

"Truly."

She threw her arm around him and kissed him so heartily, he wished he had said these things much sooner.

The kiss grew heated and yearning.

"I will do my best to be a good wife," she vowed as his lips left hers, sliding to her earlobe.

His answer was an incoherent mumble as he sucked the lobe into his mouth, then toyed with it with his tongue.

She clutched him tightly, gasping. His hand stole into her shift and found her soft breast. His thumb teased her nipple before his mouth left her ear. Slowly, he eased her shift lower, until her breast was exposed to his eager lips and tongue.

He could hear her panting now, the sound adding to his own arousal, and when she whispered his name with excitement, surprise and delight, he had never been so thrilled to hear it.

With practiced proficiency, he pushed off his boots using one foot, then the other, as he continued to pleasure her with his lips and tongue and hands. Then he slipped off his breeches, so that he was naked.

She was still separated from him by the barriers of the bedclothes and her shift. Quickly he rose from the bed. She stared at him with wide eyes as he ripped the coverings from the bed.

Her eyes desire-darkened, she tore the shift from her own body, revealing her glorious form to his hungry eyes.

She was perfect, from the top of her blond head to her toes.

He had known many women, and had liked them for their various attributes, yet if someone had asked him to describe the ideal woman, he would have described Genevieve almost exactly.

She held out her arms for him, and he needed nothing more to urge him to join her in the bed.

Again entwined in his arms, she eagerly welcomed his embrace. The sensation of his naked skin against hers was beyond anything she could have imagined. She had thought breasts had only one function; how delightful to discover otherwise.

He began to stroke her lower down, his fingers seeming to know how best to set her heart beating and her blood throbbing.

Wanting to please him as he was her, she caressed and stroked him in return, glorying in the feel of his hard muscles, the stubble on his chin, and his thick hair brushing his shoulders.

She felt his knee move between her legs.

It is there… she thought vaguely as she parted them.

Raising himself on his elbows, he gently took

her face between his palms and regarded her gravely, although his eyes burned with need and a hunger she also felt.

"It may hurt," he cautioned as his hands moved away.

Then she felt him put the tip of his manhood against her.

Staring down at her, he eased himself inside her. She gasped and squeezed her eyes shut at the sudden pain.

Then he kissed her cheeks and stroked her as he began to rock, slowly. He spoke softly, uttering quiet words of endearment that made her wonder if he was part poet.

"That is all that should hurt, and just this time," he murmured, smiling and yet concerned for her, too.

She nodded, trusting him. Wanting him, the want growing with every movement of his body.

She began to respond with the same rhythm as the pain subsided.

His breathing grew harsh and ragged, and a slick sweat coated both their bodies as the rhythm quickened.

Then, with a low growl, he thrust hard into her, the sudden sensation sending her seemingly beyond her body, to a new and wondrous place that she had no words to describe.

Panting, Dylan pressed a soft kiss on her lips. She opened her eyes to watch him as he ever so slowly pulled away.

He got up and retrieved the coverings, which had become a heap at the end of the bed. Throwing them over her, then getting beneath them, he raised himself on his elbow and smiled at her. "I wouldn't want you to be getting another chill."

She snuggled against him.

"Then you must keep me warm," she murmured.

"Gladly, wife, gladly."

She smiled happily, her head against his slowly rising and falling chest.

She had not known it would be so wonderful, she mused with a contented sigh. If she had, she would not have cast so harsh a judgment on Cecily, or even Dylan's other lovers. She could not blame them for wanting to be with her husband.

Her husband. How wonderful that sounded. Now, she was glad she had gotten into his bed at Craig Fawr, although, she thought with a merry little grin, if she had known then what she knew now, she would have wakened him as soon as she joined him.

She glanced up at his handsome face, and realized he had fallen asleep.

She continued to study him. In his sleep, he looked younger, and almost innocent. So he might have looked to his first lover. What was her name? Angharad, Trefor's mother.

At least she assumed Angharad was his first. Perhaps there had been another, when he was even younger. That seemed difficult to believe...or perhaps not.

Perhaps there had been others who had not given him a child.

It didn't matter, she told herself, for she believed what he said.

She rested her hand on her stomach and thought instead of the children *she* would gladly give him.

Raised on one elbow, Dylan watched Genevieve as she slept, her naked back to him, the rest of her hidden beneath the coverings. Her shoulder rose and fell with her deep, even breathing.

He regarded the corona of her hair, darker in the dim light. It was so soft, like her skin. His gaze traveled from there to the slope of her shoulder, the curve of it reminding him of her other womanly curves.

The early-morning light, diffused through the

linen shutter, made this seem almost a pleasant dream.

He sighed softly. This had come about in such an odd—nay, miraculous—fashion.

Yes, miraculous seemed the better word. Without expectation, without planning, without anything except, perhaps, the guidance of God, he had found a wife he could cherish.

A wife he could love.

Pleased beyond measure at that thought, he let his finger slide ever so slowly along her bare arm toward her shoulder.

She sat up abruptly, brushing at her arm, a look of panic on her face.

"I'm sorry!" he cried, distressed by her unexpected reaction even as part of his mind registered the sight of her perfect breasts. "I didn't mean to startle you."

She sighed and smiled slightly before pulling up the covers, just punishment for shocking her, he supposed.

"You are not used to sleeping with someone, no doubt," he said.

"Yes, I am."

"You are?"

"Of course. At Lady Katherine's we all had to share."

An image, terribly immoral yet incredibly arousing, momentarily boggled Dylan's mind.

Genevieve drew up her knees and wrapped her arms around them. "Once, when I was sleeping, one of the girls put a beetle on my arm."

She made a face of extreme disgust. "By the time I woke up, it was nearly at my face. I screamed and screamed. Lady Katherine came running as if her house was afire."

"Was she angry?"

Genevieve made a wry smile that utterly charmed him. "I told her I had a bad dream. And I did many times, after that. I used to dream giant beetles were chasing me. To eat me."

She shuddered, which told him he must and should put his arms around her, so he did. "That was cruel of that girl."

Genevieve shrugged. "Cecily was like that. She thought it very funny."

"Did she want you to get in trouble?"

Even the way Genevieve cocked her head to look at him delighted him this morning.

"I don't think so," she replied thoughtfully. "I don't believe Cecily thought much beyond the immediate effect. She was not a very imaginative young lady."

"She doesn't sound like my idea of a lady at all, frightening you like that."

Genevieve regarded him with some surprise, her brow furrowed. "I thought you would have been the kind of boy who often played tricks on people."

He shook his head gravely. "Not I, my lady. I was a perfect little angel."

Her expression was distinctly dubious, and he had to grin. "Well, I got into a little trouble—but only because I was such a brave, bold lad, you understand."

"Of course," she agreed, her expression grave, but her eyes twinkling merrily. "I daresay you were so brave and bold you were never punished, and your father secretly rewarded you."

Suddenly, and without a word, he got out of the warm and cozy bed. She immediately recalled what little she had heard of his past and wished she could call back her reference to his father. "Forgive me! I didn't mean to upset you."

He pulled on his breeches, and he sighed. "No, forgive *me*. I haven't told you about my father, so how could you know?"

"Lady Roanna told me a little."

"Did she? What, exactly?"

"That your father and grandfather were selfish and cruel."

"They were that."

"Were they cruel to you?"

He sat on the bed, giving her a somewhat strained and weary smile. "Thank the good Lord, they never got the chance. I never knew my father. He died before I was born."

She could think of no reply beyond leaning forward and kissing him gently.

At least, she meant it to be that way, but as always, the moment her lips met his, her passion took command. And he responded in kind.

In another moment, his breeches were again a rumpled heap on the floor beside the bed, and in the next, soft sounds of passionate desire filled the stone chamber.

"Anwyl!"

Genevieve opened her eyes to see Dylan yanking on his breeches, and slowly became aware of the oddest sound issuing from the hall below.

She sighed, still languid from making love. "What is it?"

"They're drunk, the lot of them."

She sat up rather gingerly and glanced at the window. "What o'clock is it?"

He rose and went to get his tunic. "Nearly noon, I should think. Have you ever heard such noise?"

"They should be at their work," she agreed.

He picked up his tunic and gave her a surprised look. "Work? The day after I return with a bride?"

"Yes, work. I thought that was why you were angry."

"It's the singing. Terrible! An insult to a Welsh-man's ears, like dogs howling at the moon."

"Oh."

"Will you join me for something to eat?"

"Since no one has brought us anything here, I suppose I should."

"I told Cait no one was to disturb us this morn-ing."

"Oh," she answered, blushing, as she slowly got out of bed.

It didn't help that he simply stood and watched her.

"Would you get me a shift?" she asked.

"What's wrong with the one you wore last night?" His lips turned up into a smile that was perilously close to a leer. "I like that one."

"It is too good for every day."

"But I like it," he repeated in a low, seductive tone.

"I fear every time you look at me, you will be unable to concentrate on your duties."

"You've learned something of me already," he said with mock seriousness.

"Please get me another shift," she asked as she went to the washstand.

"If you insist."

"I do. And my dark blue gown with scarlet trim, if you can find it."

She half expected him to tell her to wear that awful brown thing, but he didn't. Instead, she jumped when she felt his hands running up her arms.

"I wish you didn't have to get dressed at all," he whispered, pressing a kiss to her shoulder.

She swallowed hard. "Yes, well, it would cause quite a stir in the hall if I went down naked."

He kissed her neck. "You could stay here. In bed."

She sighed and leaned back against him. "But then my duties would be neglected."

"There hasn't been a chatelaine here since my grandmother died."

"There is now."

"No one would miss you."

She stiffened. "Would you have me stay cooped up in this room all day?"

He turned her to face him, an apologetic look on his face. "Only joking, me. I meant no offense." He smiled his charming smile. "I fear I am a selfish beast. I want to keep you all to myself."

It was hard to be angry at him when he looked at her that way. "As long as you were only teasing. I want to be a proper chatelaine, Dylan. That's what I was taught to do."

He kissed her lightly on the forehead. "I'm sure you will be."

"Did you get my shift?"

He smote himself on the forehead and reeled backward. "*Anwyl*, it slipped my mind! Right away, my lady."

"You'll fall and hurt yourself!" she chided, trying not to laugh, which would surely only encourage his antics.

"I am too nimble."

He started to do what might have been a jig, but he stumbled into the stool. He almost tripped over it, yet managed to right himself before she could help him.

"See?" he said, panting. "Like a tumbler I am."

"I would not try to make my living at such arts,

if I were you. Now I had better get my garments myself, and you can see to your howling dogs.''

"Aye, they've got to be silenced," he agreed, his tone serious and his eyes laughing. "Adieu for now, Genevieve."

"Adieu, oh nimble one."

Chapter Nine

Dylan sauntered toward the men, or at least those who were still awake and singing. More than a few lay sleeping, their heads on the table, and some in puddles of spilled ale.

Dylan shook his head at the waste, while those still conscious spotted him and mercifully fell silent.

Thomas, whose skinny legs looked incapable of holding him upright at the best of times, rose unsteadily and peered at Dylan somewhat doubtfully. "My lord?"

"Aye, who else? What was that you were moaning? A dirge?"

Thomas frowned. "A ballad."

"Really? It didn't sound like any ballad I've ever heard."

The men scowled as they glanced at each other.

"It's the one the baron made on his way home from the Crusade," Thomas reported.

"You make it sound like the poor man died in a thousand agonies. I would save your singing for when you are sober if you are going to sound so bad when you're drunk."

"A celebration it was," one of the men mumbled.

"I know you were celebrating—but must my Norman wife have such an introduction to Welsh music?"

"Ah!" The men sighed with sudden understanding.

"Ah, indeed," Dylan replied. "So no more singing until you can do it right, is it?"

They all nodded.

"Now then, Thomas, where is Llannulid?"

"At home, I expect."

"Fetch her here. I would have her show Genevieve about the castle."

"Aye, my lord."

As Thomas started toward the door, his staggering steps gave Dylan a moment's pause.

"Thomas, perhaps—"

"No, no, my lord, it is only that the ground is slanted just by here," Thomas explained thickly.

It was no more slanted than the rest of the floor, but Dylan let the matter pass. "The rest of you, go to sleep. You're no good to me like this. I trust the sentries are not drunk."

"Drunk, my lord?" a thickset fellow named Ifor answered dubiously. "No...not drunk."

But not completely sober, either, Dylan thought without rancor. He could not be too angry. They had been celebrating his wedding, after all.

So he strolled toward the kitchen. He was starving and the smell of fresh bread coming from there made his stomach growl like a baited bear.

He entered the enormous room dominated by a large hearth used for roasting meat or cooking soups and stews in big iron pots. At one side were the ovens made of bricks and with iron doors.

To his surprise, only one person was there working, and that was Elidan, who baked the bread and pastries. She was a broad woman of soft flesh, as if she were made of dough herself.

"Where is everybody?" he asked, coming to the flour-covered table where Elidan was kneading a huge mound of dough.

Some loaves were already cooling there, and he helped himself to one.

"In bed yet," she replied, scarcely glancing at him.

"My wife will want something to eat."

Elidan nodded at the cooling loaves. "There's them."

"She may want more than that."

"Then I'll need help."

"Fetch it."

Elidan glanced up. "Now?"

"I suppose I can rouse them."

Elidan nodded and went back to her kneading. "She's a Norman," she remarked as he went to the door, "so I don't know what kind of bread she'll like."

Dylan turned back as Elidan raised her substantial fist and punched down the bread. Although muffled by the quantity of dough, the blow nevertheless made an impressive thud.

"Bread is bread," Dylan answered with a shrug.

Again Elidan's fist rose and fell. "She probably only likes the finest flour, ground white as snow, I am thinking."

"This is excellent bread, Elidan. I'm sure it will be good enough for her."

"I hope she agrees with you, my lord."

"She will," he assured her.

As he went out in search of the kitchen boys and serving maids, he hoped he had not just told a lie.

And he wondered if Elidan was always so rough with her dough.

"So, repeat it to them again," Genevieve instructed Llannulid later that day as they stood in the hall together, facing the female servants. "The bread and butter, then the wine, then the roast meats or stews, then the fruit. It is as simple as that."

Llannulid nodded her understanding and spoke in Welsh. The servants gave one another subtle, sidelong glances.

"Do they not understand?"

"Yes, my lady, they understood," Llannulid answered in her high, musical voice.

All the women had lovely voices, Genevieve reflected. She had not heard one that grated on the ear. "Good. I shall expect this order of service at every meal. If there are more than the usual courses, I will instruct them as necessary."

Making what she thought of as a "Lady Katherine" smile—small and perhaps a little condescending, to show who was in charge—Genevieve faced the women again.

After Llannulid finished speaking, Genevieve waved her hand to indicate that the servants were free to go. They moved off toward the kitchen, whispering among themselves. As they left, Genevieve noticed Gwethalyn sitting on a stool nearby, watching.

The little girl had been following her and Llannulid about all day. That wouldn't have been a problem, in and of itself; unfortunately, the child possessed the most unnerving stare Genevieve had ever encountered.

No, that was not quite right. Gwethalyn had her father's intensity. As disturbing as it was in him, it was distinctly upsetting in one so young.

"I think perhaps we have done enough for today," Genevieve said, suddenly very tired.

She had spent the whole day exploring the castle and its storerooms. Her husband was obviously a prosperous lord, yet it was as if the castle were being run by children. Goods and foodstuffs were piled anywhere and everywhere in the storerooms, with no order or reason. A thief could probably make off with half of it before anybody realized anything was missing.

Llannulid nodded and called for her daughter.

Gwethalyn hurried toward them and took hold of her mother's hand, still staring at Genevieve.

Llannulid looked from her daughter to Genevieve and an apologetic smile appeared on her face. "Forgive her, my lady. She stares because she thinks you are a princess and nothing I say can change her mind.''

''It's all right,'' Genevieve assured her, for that was an undeniably flattering mistake.

She gave Llannulid a sidelong glance. ''She reminds me very much of her father, except for her hair.''

''Yes, she is very like him,'' Llannulid replied evenly. ''The hair is like my mother's.''

Genevieve wished she had kept her mouth shut and turned away—to see a tall, statuesque, dark-haired woman standing near the entrance. The stranger wore a simple homespun gown, with the sleeves rolled up to her elbows, revealing rather muscular forearms. Her face was strong-featured, yet not unattractive. Or rather, it might have been attractive if she had looked less hostile.

Amazon. The word popped into Genevieve's head, and she recalled hearing about the women warriors. It was very easy to imagine this woman with sword or bow.

The woman addressed Llannulid in Welsh, although her eyes never left Genevieve.

Genevieve stepped forward and said, with not a little scorn for the woman's impertinence, ''Llannulid, who is this?''

"I am Angharad," the woman replied in very good French.

Although she hadn't moved, Genevieve felt as if she had stumbled. After Llannulid, she had not expected the mothers of Dylan's other children to be so...imposing.

What was Arthur's mother like—another Boadicea, or like Llannulid?

She told herself it didn't matter, because she was Dylan's wife. "Is there something you require?"

With a smug smile on her face, Angharad shook her head. "No, my lady. Only wanting to see you, I was."

"Why?"

Genevieve's imperious tone brought a wary look to Angharad's eyes, and she was glad to see it. This woman had best remember to whom she spoke. Genevieve was no peasant, but a highborn lady who was married to this woman's lord.

Unfortunately, the wary look didn't last beyond a moment. "Wanting to see Dylan's wife, is all."

"Since you have seen me, you may go. You may leave, too, Llannulid."

With a sniff, Angharad turned on her heel and marched toward the door. Llannulid and Gwethalyn trotted after her.

Angharad was about to pull open the door when it suddenly burst open.

"Mair!" Angharad chided as another young woman entered—or, it seemed, danced—into the hall.

Shaking her head, Angharad continued outside, still followed by Llannulid and Gwethalyn, who gave the stranger a brief, but friendly, greeting.

Mair. She had heard that before. Was it a word—or a name?

Suddenly Genevieve remembered. This was Arthur's mother.

Genevieve clasped her hands together and prayed for patience as Mair pranced closer. She was pretty in a common sort of way, with thick, curling brown hair and freckles scattered across her nose.

Was there no type or form of woman that did not have some appeal for Dylan DeLanyea? Genevieve wondered crossly.

Mair came to a halt and surveyed Genevieve with a matter-of-fact curiosity that was only slightly easier to bear than Angharad's hostility, Llannulid's sympathy and Gwethalyn's awe.

"So, you are the Lady Genevieve," she announced cheerfully.

"I am."

"I am Mair, Arthur's mother. He told me you were pretty and I must say, you are."

"Thank you."

Mair laughed merrily, the sound like the trill of a bird after a long and silent winter. "Angharad was her most Angharad-y, I think. I hope she didn't upset you too much."

Genevieve drew herself up proudly. "She did not upset me at all."

"Really? You *are* some woman, then. Angharad can be cold as ice, her, and about as cheery as an early frost," she went on with a broad smile. "She likes to lord it over the rest of us because she gave Dylan his first son."

"You gave him his second."

"Well, he says so. I have my doubts."

Genevieve was too dumbfounded to respond, and Mair laughed again. "*Anwyl,* I told him it could just as easily be Morvyrn's, or Lloyd's, or possibly Tewdwer's. But he insists Arthur is his, and if a baron wants to take the credit for my son, who am I to say no?"

Genevieve had heard tales of great storms at sea, with roaring winds and huge waves. She felt rather as if she were in one as Mair looked around the hall.

"I told him he should get married. Glad I am he finally took my advice."

"Your advice?"

Mair grinned. "Mine and about a hundred other people's, I suppose."

She dropped onto one of the benches and patted the wood beside her for Genevieve to join her, as if this would be the most natural thing in the world.

"It's almost time for the evening meal," Genevieve prevaricated.

It was possible for Mair to frown.

"Oh," she said, putting her hands on her knees as a prelude to rising.

Reconsidering, Genevieve quickly gestured for her to stay seated. "There is a little while yet. I don't even know where Dylan is at the moment."

"At the *ffridd*, him."

"The freeth?" Genevieve repeated, trying to pronounce the word properly.

"Aye. A pen for the sheep, that is. They're making sure it's ready for the gathering."

"Oh."

Mair gave her a friendly smile. "A bit much, is it?"

Genevieve nodded.

"That's what happens when you marry so fast."

Genevieve gave her a wary, sidelong look, wondering what she knew.

"We've all got to get used to it, I suppose. Him just off to visit his uncle for a celebration, he says, and he comes back in a week with a wife."

She gave Genevieve an approving smile. "That's why I think you must be quite a woman."

Genevieve flushed hotly. "He charmed me right from the first."

"Of course he did. That's what Dylan DeLanyea does."

"You don't seem to mind."

Mair's laugh filled the hall, and Genevieve saw Cait peering from the kitchen corridor.

"Tell the servants we shall prepare for the evening meal in a little while," Genevieve ordered. "I'll call you from the kitchen when it's time."

Cait nodded and disappeared.

"I thought she'd be next, myself," Mair mused aloud.

She glanced at Genevieve. "No need to look like that. Cait's a grown woman, and if she didn't want to, that would be the end of it. Chivalrous is Dylan, and no mistake."

"He didn't tell me about you or the others."

Mair's brow furrowed with puzzlement. "Why not?"

"You'll have to ask him that question."

"I will," she replied in a tone that made it very clear that she would.

"Perhaps you shouldn't," Genevieve replied, suddenly doubtful.

"Oh, I can ask him. He'll probably say we slipped his mind, but I won't believe it for a second. He probably thought you wouldn't marry him if you knew, being a Norman."

"He would have been right."

"There, then!"

"You cannot say you think he was right to keep his children a secret."

Mair shook her head. "No, not right, exactly, but it's understandable if he wanted you enough to marry you and thought you would refuse because of them. He must be mad in love with you."

Genevieve flushed, then gave Mair another side-long glance. "Was he mad in love with you?"

"Not a bit. Nor me with him, and neither one of us ever claimed otherwise."

Mair regarded her with steadfast frankness. "Angharad acts like a queen because she was his first, but she knew he would never marry her. She's not a noble, for one thing. For another, he was too young to decide when he went with her. Me, I had both eyes open, and there's never been a more attractive man, to my thinking, so I suggested we become lovers.''

"*You* suggested?''

''Why not? He was willing, so was I. That's enough.''

''But you had other lovers?''

''Oh, *anwyl*, yes! I like men.''

''Obviously'' was on the tip of Genevieve's tongue, but she refrained from saying it.

Mair grew serious. ''Llannulid was a little different. You've noticed she speaks your tongue very well?''

''So do you,'' Genevieve replied.

''Do you think so?'' Mair cried happily.

Then she returned to her graver manner. ''Not as well as Llannulid, though. She was raised by the Normans, in the south. Dylan went to visit an earl there and brought her back with him. Eight months later, Gwethalyn was born. By then, Llannulid wasn't with him anymore. Dylan had got her a little house in the village.''

''She was recently married to the steward?''

Mair laughed. ''Aye, to Thomas-y-Tenau—Skinny Thomas, that is.''

Genevieve smiled. ''He is rather thin.''

''Thin?'' Mair guffawed. ''I'm always afraid a good stiff breeze will take him straight to heaven.''

"What is his real name?"

"Skinny Thomas."

"No, I mean his Christian name."

"Thomas. We have to add something, or we might get him mixed up with Thomas the smith, or Thomas the shepherd from over the hill."

"Oh."

Suddenly Mair jumped up as if she had spied a snake on the floor by her foot.

"*Anwyl,* here they come, and me not got the ale off the cart," she cried.

Genevieve could hear the sounds of men talking and laughing outside, too, and likewise rose in dismay, albeit with less energy. She had talked too long. The tables were not even set up!

Mair smiled again, and there was genuine sincerity in her frank brown eyes. "I wish you every happiness. Just be a little patient with him, and with us, and we'll try to be patient with you. Remember, he's had lovers, but it's you he married—and remind Angharad of that if you have to!"

With that, Mair danced toward the entrance just as a gaggle of men entered, Dylan at their head.

He had been a long time outside. His hair was ruffled from the breeze, and his face ruddy.

He paused when he saw Genevieve, a little smile on his face.

How lovely she looked, this wife of his, with her fluffy blond curls and blue eyes. She stood in his hall like a queen, a worthy wife for a baron, a fitting chatelaine for his castle, one that any Norman would envy.

Then, with a start, he realized boisterous, bold Mair was there.

She came toward him, a knowing smile on her face as she punched him on the arm.

"Keeping secrets from her, you were," Mair chided merrily in Welsh. "No wonder she looks as dazed as a mole in sunlight. And here I was thinking it was just your prowess that overwhelmed her."

"Greetings, Mair," Dylan replied, trying not to sound annoyed. "I wondered if that was your cart in my courtyard."

"Aye, and I had best see to the unloading."

Her gaze momentarily followed his men as they wandered into the hall. "Your men look like they're barely alive. Must have been quite a celebration—and you didn't invite me."

"I forgot."

She laughed without bitterness. "I'll say you did, but I can see why. A beauty she is, for a Norman. Proud like a Norman, too."

"I think we'll be needing that ale."

"Right enough. All your barrels will be empty now, I'm sure. Good day to you, then, my lord, and best wishes on your marriage."

She went to go past him, and he started toward Genevieve.

Mair hesitated a moment beside him.

"Angharad was by to say hello," she whispered.

Chapter Ten

Dylan was relieved to notice that Genevieve seemed too busy with the details of setting up the tables to pay much heed to him, and he swiftly hurried toward their bedchamber. He would wash and dress in a clean tunic before returning to the hall.

Thus refreshed, he would surely feel more up to the task of talking about Angharad. And Mair. And Llannulid.

Once in the bedchamber, he drew off his tunic and splashed cold water over his face and shoulders. At least the *ffridd* needed no repair, and they could begin gathering the sheep tomorrow. All those on the mountain could be brought down, and those about to have lambs separated from the rest of the flock. The winter had not been a harsh one, so he could be optimistic about a healthy and growing herd.

He heard the door open and raised his head, squinting to see as the water ran over his eyes. "Genevieve?"

"Yes."

He reached for a square of linen and dried off his face, taking his time about it.

"I came to apologize," she said in a small voice.

He threw down the linen and faced her. To his surprise, she looked quite upset. "What for?"

"I did not have the hall prepared and now you will have to wait to eat. Forgive me."

He grinned. "Is that all? I assure you, I can wait a while."

The tension ebbed from her shoulders. "Truly?"

"Truly."

He frowned with mock consternation. "Just make sure such a terrible thing never happens again."

She didn't smile and he went to her, taking her hands in his and regarding her tenderly. "It is not so serious, Genevieve. I am not used to having my food ready the moment I come into the hall."

She didn't look particularly mollified. "That doesn't mean I should have been so remiss."

"There is no need to chastise yourself, either. This is but your first day here. I have remembered that, if you have not."

"I wanted everything to be properly done," she mumbled.

He put his knuckle under her chin and made her look up at him. "Is this a pout I am seeing?"

She shrugged.

"It is a pout, and I know of one good way to get rid of it," he whispered, bending to kiss her.

His arms tightened about her as he gave himself up to the enjoyment of tasting her lips and slipping his tongue into the enfolding warmth of her mouth.

All too soon, however, she pulled away. "We should go down. They will be waiting for us."

"Let them wait," he murmured, tugging her close again.

This time, she turned her head away.

"Genevieve, they can wait."

"But that is not—"

"What Normans do?"

"Very well. It is not what proper Normans do."

"I am not a proper Norman."

"I...I know that."

He regarded her suspiciously. "Is it Angharad and Mair? Did they upset you?"

She turned away and walked toward the window. "You can't expect that I wouldn't find them rather…disconcerting."

"Angharad especially, eh?" he said warily. "She can be…difficult."

Genevieve glanced back at him over her shoulder. "Yet you must have cared for her once."

"And I like her still. She is the mother of my firstborn son, too, so I am bound to respect her."

"Of course."

"Would you like me to speak to her?"

"No. I must learn to deal with…all this… myself."

In truth, he was rather relieved to hear that. "What did Mair say to you? She's got a tongue on her, that one, but no guile at all."

"Yes, I agree."

"Genevieve, look at me."

Reluctantly, she obeyed, and he saw something in her eyes that made him speak gently, and sincerely. "I know it is not going to be easy for you for the first while. And I know I have given you much to endure, in your mind, at least. Let us be patient with each other."

"That is what Mair said."

"She can be quite wise, when she's not being impertinent."

He went to Genevieve and put his hands on her

shoulders, regarding her steadily. "I want us to be happy, and I think we can be, if we let the past be the past and look to the future. *Our* future."

She smiled tentatively. "I will try."

"Good. Now of course we cannot keep people waiting, so we had best go down."

"I trust you intend to put a tunic on?" she asked, and he was delighted to see the spark of mischief in her eyes.

"Maybe not. Sometimes the Welsh eat half-naked."

Her eyes widened and his laugh echoed off the walls. "Not savages, the Welsh. Only teasing I was."

"I hoped you were."

"It's true you are getting to know me better," he said as he went to a chest to get a new tunic.

"Soon I will know everything about you."

He looked at her and smiled that slow, seductive smile. "And I will know everything about you."

She went toward him, drawn by an irresistible urge.

"Perhaps," she said in a whisper made hoarse by desire, "perhaps they can wait below for a little while, if we are swift."

He laughed softly and tugged her into his arms.

* * *

Genevieve had never suspected a man could be *that* swift.

Then again, she knew very little of men in general, and was only slowly learning about her amazing husband.

Seated at the high table, she sighed contentedly, although her contentment lasted only a moment before she began to scrutinize the servants to ensure that they were performing their tasks as she expected of them.

In general, they were. Some of the women could have moved more smartly—and they might have, if Dylan and the other men didn't seem to feel it necessary to speak to them so often, and in such flirtatious tones.

Especially Dylan, who at this very instant was waylaying Cait with some sort of Welsh nonsense, to judge by his bantering tone.

He had not said one word about how she had arranged the tables in a much more orderly fashion that made the serving easier and faster, or noted how the food arrived in proper order.

"Do you require something of her, my lord?" Genevieve asked.

He barely gave his wife a glance. "No. Just asking after her family. Her father's an expert at lamb-

ing and I wanted to make sure he would be able
to come if we need him."

"Oh." Genevieve took a bite of the coarse bread
and tried to chew it without opening her mouth,
something not particularly easy.

"What's the matter?"

"The bread—I am going to have to take bites
the size of a pea."

His brow furrowed as he looked at her. "You
like it, don't you?"

"It's tasty enough, just coarse."

"I see."

"Do all your men flirt with the serving women
all the time?"

"They're not flirting. They're talking. Not
standing on rank, us—and I like it that way."

Genevieve could not ignore his tone of finality,
or the annoyed look in his eyes as he looked at
her. "I suppose you think I was flirting with
Cait?"

She blushed hotly and stared down at the bread.

He smiled. "God's holy heart, woman, I will
have to become a mute to keep you from being
jealous, I think."

She gave him a sidelong glance, mindful of his
words that he intended to abide by his marriage

vows, and suddenly ashamed of her jealous heart. "I'm trying not to be."

"Good."

"Tomorrow, I would like to rearrange the store-rooms."

"Fine. Do as you will with the household. It's yours to command."

"I thought I should try to get some finer flour."

"If you like."

"Can we afford French wine?"

"I think so. Ask Thomas."

"I would like to take a count of the linen."

Dylan turned to his wife, who sat so upright and rigid at the table, as stiff-backed as any Norman noble he had ever encountered, and quite different from the woman he had so recently made love to. Surely she could not still be doubting his intention to be faithful to her. "Do whatever you see fit. You are the chatelaine here. I have confidence in your abilities."

"But you are the master. I should have your permission."

He grinned. "Master, eh? I like that. So you must do *whatever* I say?"

She lowered her eyes demurely and blushed prettily. "Yes."

"Well, well, well, I shall have to see what I can think of."

She raised her eyes and looked at him. "That also means I cannot make decisions without your approval."

Dylan waved his hand dismissively. "Perhaps that is what Lady Katherine taught you, but we shall not have such strictness here. You can do what you like—within reason, of course."

"But how will I know what you consider 'within reason'?"

She had him there, and he had to admit it. "Very well, Genevieve. For the first little while, I suppose you will have to consult with me."

"Good."

He cocked his head to one side. "What else is troubling you?"

"Nothing, my lord," she replied, and yet he didn't quite believe her.

"Are you sure?"

"Nothing important."

Before he could press her further, Thomas rose from his place. "If you please, my lord, we were so ashamed this morning at your criticism, we want to sing now for you and your lovely bride."

Dylan smiled happily. "By all means, if you can

sing something more pleasant than that cats' howling I heard before.''

The men grumbled in protest, until Thomas held up his hand. ''Now then, boys, none of that. We'll prove him wrong with our song.''

''What's happening?'' Genevieve asked.

''My men are going to sing to us.''

''But the meal's not finished.''

''No matter.''

He thought she made a derisive sound, but when he looked at her, he couldn't really read her expression.

Then he told himself if she was a little put out, that was all right. He wanted to hear the song his men were going to sing, for he was quite certain they had made it up today as a retaliation for his insult.

To his vast amusement, he learned he was quite right, and that he had underestimated their capacity for bawdy lyrics. He was suddenly glad Genevieve couldn't understand a word of Welsh, or her proper Norman sensibilities would have been horrified.

Not that he had a lot of sympathy for her proper Norman sensibilities; he just didn't want her upset any more. To be honest, he had underestimated how difficult it might be for her to be comfortable at Beaufort, and he did want her to be comfortable, and happy.

But she would have to get over this insistence on rules and schedules. That was not his way, and never would be. He wanted his people to be happy and carefree in a way they had not been under his father and his grandfather. He would not be some sort of petty tyrant, so he never insisted on strict times and ways of doing things. As long as the work was done, that was all that mattered.

When their song was concluded, with a rousing chorus that described Dylan's manhood in the most exaggerated and colorful terms possible, Dylan shoved back his chair.

"Where are you going? We have not had the fruit!" Genevieve protested.

"I'm not leaving. I am responding," he explained.

Using the same tune and repeating some of the words, he proceeded to sing his own song, referring to a particularly enthusiastic ram instead of himself. The men laughed and clapped, and by the time he was finished, Dylan was rather pleased with himself.

He flopped down into his chair and grinned broadly.

"What was that about?" Genevieve asked somewhat dubiously.

"A ram," he answered innocently enough.

"You could have been a wandering entertainer performing for your supper."

"Do you think so?" he asked, delighted, until he got a look at her censorious face.

"If you will excuse me, I believe I shall retire," she said, rising haughtily.

His good humor ruined, he sarcastically said, "We haven't had the fruit yet."

"I don't want any. Good night."

With that, she swept out of the hall, and every person there knew she was angry.

Dylan put a wry smile on his face. "She's a Norman."

Everyone chuckled, and soon enough, they were all singing about love and honor.

While up in her bedchamber, feeling that all her efforts were unappreciated, all her desire to be a good wife not important to him, and all the people below barely civilized, Genevieve sat and stared out the window at the moon.

"Genevieve?" Dylan whispered as he crept into their bed later that night. "Are you awake?"

Her back to him, she didn't answer.

"Genevieve, are you awake?" he repeated, stroking her arm.

"What do you want?" she demanded softly—and angrily, pulling the coverings around herself tightly so that he couldn't caress her anymore.

"I knew you were awake."

"I'm *trying* to sleep."

"*I'm* trying to apologize."

She rolled over and looked at him. "You are?"

"It was just a jesting song, Genevieve. There was no need for you to get so upset."

"Your behavior was hardly dignified."

"Do you want to hear it?"

Of all the things he might have said, she had not expected this. "I wouldn't understand the words."

"I can translate as I sing," he offered with a cunning smile that was very hard to resist.

In fact, it was irresistible. "Very well."

Dylan obediently began to sing, censuring some of the more lewd portions, just to be safe.

After a moment, Genevieve started to smile, and once or twice, she giggled—a very delightful sound in the darkness of their bedchamber.

"Was that anything so very terrible?" he asked when he was finished.

"No—but I don't think that was an exact translation."

"My lady!"

"My husband!" she cried, mimicking his feigned dismay.

"Well, some things do not translate exactly," he explained somewhat truthfully.

"I know, and I fear you are even more vain than I thought, to make up a song like that about yourself and your...body."

"It's not about me."

She laughed skeptically, then snuggled closer to him. "You do have a lovely voice, you know."

"Then I shall sing you another song, shall I?"

"Like that?"

"No," he whispered softly. "A song for lovers."

And when he finished singing the beautiful song in his fine, rich voice, they made a different kind of music.

Genevieve awoke the next morning in the dim light of early dawn and realized Dylan was already up and moving about their bedchamber. "What are you doing?"

He gave her a smile as he continued to dress. "It is a fine morning to gather the sheep."

"Mair said you would be doing that."

"Did she now? Well, a long day it will be, so

do not look for us to be finished before the sun sets.''

"You, too?" she asked, surprised, for she had assumed that whatever the task, he would only supervise.

"Of course. I take the highest place in the line. Have for years."

Although she wasn't sure what he was talking about, she heard the pride in his voice, and knew that the "highest place in the line" was important to him. "What line?" she asked, shifting into a sitting position so she could see him better.

He sat on the end of the bed to put on his boots. "We make a line up the mountain, the men and the dogs, and then we swing down toward the *ffridd*, gathering the sheep as we go."

"Oh." It didn't sound like a proper job for a baron, but he seemed to think it was, so she would be silent.

"What will you do all day?" he asked, twisting to look at her.

"I told you last night. The storerooms are completely disorganized. I shall have them sorted out, washed and arranged properly."

He nodded. "Ah, yes. You will need Llannulid, then. I'll tell Thomas."

Genevieve hugged her knees as she regarded his

broad back. "She speaks French very well. Mair told me a little bit about her."

Again, Dylan looked at her over his shoulder. "What did Mair tell you?"

"That you brought Llannulid back with you after you visited a Norman nobleman, she had Gwethalyn eight months later, but by then you had given Llannulid her own house in the village."

"Is that all?"

"Yes."

He rose and came to sit beside her, taking her hand in his. "I am going to tell you this because I trust you, Genevieve, but you are not to tell another soul. Will you promise to keep this confidence, since it is Llannulid's more than mine?"

Confused and rather dismayed by the seriousness of his tone, Genevieve nodded her agreement.

"Good." He sighed softly. "Gwethalyn is not my child."

"Not yours? Then why—"

He put his finger gently to her lips. "I never actually claimed her as mine. I simply never said she was not, and if people assume that she is, I let them."

"In the woods you told me all three children were yours."

"I confess I was annoyed with you then, so I

was a little less than honest, but in a way, I think of her as mine, even if she is not the child of my body. I went to visit a Norman nobleman, Pierre de Grieuxville, who had recently been granted a castle and estate in the March. I was supposed to get a measure of the man—and that did not take long. He hated the Welsh with a passion, except when he loved them against their will. That beast raped Llannulid.''

There was a look of such animosity on Dylan's normally cheerful face that she could almost pity the man who engendered it.

Genevieve thought of gentle Llannulid. She knew how wonderfully intimate love could be; she could scarcely imagine that intimacy turned to violence and degradation. Tears of sympathy filled her eyes and she grasped his hand tightly.

''She came to me in the night and begged me to help her,'' Dylan continued grimly. ''I was all for killing him, myself, but she feared his men would go on a vengeful rampage.

''So I brought her away with me and told my uncle about Pierre.''

A wry smile came to his face. ''De Grieuxville probably never would have believed that he could be ousted by a single letter from a Welsh baron.''

''But he was.''

"Oh, aye, within a month he was removed from the estate and sent packing back to France."

"Meanwhile, Llannulid was here."

"Yes, in this bedchamber and supposedly as my lover, but I never touched her."

"Does her husband know the truth?"

"I expect so."

"Dylan?"

"Yes?"

"Will you forgive me for ever thinking you a completely selfish rascal?"

He reached out to caress her cheek. "In some things, I am selfish."

She turned her head to kiss the palm of his hand. "I can hardly wait to bear your child."

"Nothing would make me happier, Genevieve," he whispered as he brushed back her curls with his other hand. "Unfortunately, this morning I cannot linger, or we won't finish before dark."

"Go to your duties and leave me to do mine," she said with a smile. "I will have your meal ready when you return."

He nodded, gave her another smile and left the room, while she sighed and snuggled back under the covers for a little while, to envision how happy they both would be the day she gave him a son. Or even a daughter.

* * *

Griffydd DeLanyea, who was known for the inscrutability of his countenance, was nevertheless making no secret of his feelings as he rode toward Beaufort with his father that morning.

Some ways behind, among the other men, was Trystan, and it was of him that Griffydd spoke. "I do not think it was wise to let him come."

The baron regarded his eldest son coolly. "Why? He has helped with the gathering other years when he was home."

"That was different."

"Why?"

"Surely I don't have to say it."

"I think you do."

"That was before Dylan was married to Genevieve Perronet. You saw the way Trystan looked at her."

"Yes, I did. But as he is my son, and a knight, I have faith that he will remember she is married to another and bring no dishonor to our family."

"I trust you are right."

"Do you think keeping him from her will cool his ardor?"

"It might."

The baron shook his head. "I am not so certain.

Let him see her as Dylan's wife, happy in her own home, loving her husband.''

"You seem confident that they will love each other."

The baron gave his son a rueful smile. "Whether they're willing to admit it or not, they were half in love before they were married, or neither one of them would have agreed. Knowing Dylan, I daresay they've smoothed over the rough spots."

"I hope you're right."

"And I wish you'd stop seeing problems everywhere. Trystan is young. He will get over this infatuation soon enough, provided she is not kept from him like some kind of forbidden fruit."

"I suppose."

"I know it," the baron said with a confident smile.

Which, unfortunately, was not entirely sincere.

Chapter Eleven

Later that day, as the sun set behind the hills, Genevieve waited expectantly for Dylan and his men to return.

For possibly the hundredth time she surveyed the hall, making certain all was prepared. The tables were freshly washed and the high table sported a fine linen cloth she had discovered at the very back of a shelf in one of the dustier storerooms. She had also discovered three saltcellars that now sat ready to be used, and to divide the tables closest to the dais. She would have to ask Dylan who deserved to sit above the salt. Thomas, she was fairly sure, but other than that, she could hardly begin to guess.

The maidservants stood in the kitchen corridor ready to bring the bread and butter the moment she nodded her head.

Stifling a yawn, Genevieve wondered how much longer the men would be. She had had a very busy day sorting out the disarray, and that had only been two storerooms, albeit the ones she considered the worst. Tomorrow, she would have to begin on another.

Then she would have to learn about the castle laundry.

She grimaced as the twinge of a cramp assailed her. Usually that was a warning that her menses was about to begin. Today, she hoped it meant something else.

Finally hearing some commotion in the courtyard that she thought heralded the men's return, she adjusted her cap and veil, then smoothed down her skirt. Tonight she wore a gown of red wool with a simple leather girdle. Her cap was likewise red, her veil white. She knew the garments suited her, and she wanted very much to look pretty for Dylan.

She discerned his merry voice among the others and her heart started to beat with both happiness and anticipation, for surely he would notice her improvements in the hall tonight.

At last he entered, and she smiled brightly, admiring him anew—until she realized his uncle and cousins were with him.

He had not told her to expect such important guests! How could he have been so remiss? They would surely have to stay the night, for it was too late to return to Craig Fawr.

A hundred thoughts, all in Lady Katherine's admonishing tones, seemed to shout in her head at once as she waited for them to approach. Where would they sleep? Did she have enough clean linen? Was the food going to be fine enough? Did they have sufficient wine?

And overpowering them all was the firm conviction that Dylan should have told her of their impending arrival, so she could be properly prepared and not have to experience this sudden panic.

"Greetings, my lord," Genevieve said, coming forward, a vision of loveliness.

Despite her smiling countenance, however, Dylan knew his wife well enough by now to recognize the annoyance in her eyes.

Because they were late? He had forewarned her of that.

Perhaps Angharad had been for another visit. Later, when he was alone with Genevieve, he would ask her what had upset her, and if Angharad was the reason, he would speak with Trefor's mother, no matter whether Genevieve wanted him to or not.

For now, and despite his utter exhaustion, he smiled brightly, determined to do his best to cheer her.

Then he realized she was looking not at him, but at the baron.

"A delight to see you again, my lady," the baron said in his own charming way.

She looked at his cousins. "Welcome to our hall."

Then, finally, she gave her husband a sickly-sweet smile before addressing the baron again. "I hope you will forgive us any lack, but I was not informed of your visit."

So, there it was. She was annoyed that he hadn't told her of the baron's arrival, as if his uncle would expect to be treated like visiting royalty.

"Not standing on such formalities, us," the baron replied. "We came to help with the gathering because the weather was good. If it were not, we would not."

"Will you join us at the high table?"

"There seems to be plenty of room," the baron observed with a chuckle, "so of course we will."

"Now, we are all weary, so let us sit and eat," Dylan declared, striding forward and taking Genevieve firmly by the elbow.

He steered her toward the high table.

"No need to be in a fuss," he hissed. "These are my relatives, not the king."

"You should have told me they might be coming. I don't know where they will sleep."

"In the hall, like they always do."

"As if they were common soldiers?"

"Aye, or old friends and not spoiled, arrogant Normans."

By now, they had reached the dais. Genevieve forcefully pulled away from his grasp. "Your uncle must have the chair. I will sit beside the baron on the bench, you on his other side, and your cousins will be on either side of us."

"They'll sit where they like."

"No," she insisted quietly, and yet with unexpected decisiveness. "That is the right way, and I will have it done right in my hall."

"*My* hall."

A frown crossed her features. "Our hall."

He scanned the gathering. "Where is Father Paulus?"

"He seems to have…left us."

His eyes narrowed.

"It was not my doing," she whispered defensively. "No one has been able to find him—and all his possessions are gone from his quarters. I told you he was not a proper priest."

"Maybe he sensed he was not welcome here," Dylan growled in response.

Nevertheless, he could well believe that her instincts regarding the priest—or whatever he was—were correct. After all, he had never sought a confirmation, but accepted Father Paulus's history as the man told it to him.

But Genevieve turned away before he could reply and proceeded to tell the baron—the baron!—where he ought to sit, and then his cousins.

Fortunately, the baron looked more amused than annoyed at her presumption, Griffydd looked the way he always did, which was to say with all the expression of a stone, but Trystan, who had maneuvered his way to the place beside her with a subtlety that would have done credit to Dylan himself, looked at Dylan's wife in a way that sent a javelin of jealousy straight into his heart and all thoughts of fraudulent holy men into the ether.

If Trystan had not been his cousin, and no matter how tired Dylan was, he would have challenged him to a fight for daring to look at his wife like that.

Instead, he said nothing and allowed the meal to proceed as it normally would after his uncle made a brief blessing in Father Paulus's stead. He talked and joked, joined in the usual banter with his uncle, chastised the glum-faced Griffydd as he always did, addressed his wife when necessary—and was acutely aware of everything she, and Trystan, did.

For Genevieve's part, she seemed far more concerned with the serving of the food than the few things Trystan had to say. As for Trystan, he scarce said ten words.

Dylan wished he had spent more time in the young man's company on those occasions when he had returned to Craig Fawr. He recalled that Trystan had always been a rather reticent person, yet never so quiet as this. Perhaps he had merely grown more like the quiet Griffydd as he had aged.

Or perhaps he found it difficult to speak to a beautiful woman, especially if his feelings went beyond the familial.

Then, as a dish of apples was set before him by a very subdued Cait, Genevieve rose and addressed him, and the rest of the high table. "If you will excuse me, my lords, I shall see to your accommodation."

"Oh, the hall will do for us, my lady," the baron said. "And it is far too early for you to rob us of your presence."

"I begin to understand where my husband learned to be so charming," Genevieve replied with a smile. "However, I would feel remiss in my responsibilities if I allowed that, so I must beg you to allow me to find you suitable quarters.''

"She takes her duties very seriously," Dylan added.

"Then far be it from me to make her feel remiss," the baron answered. "Perhaps you will join us again when you are finished, my lady."

She gave a barely perceptible shake of her head. "I fear I am very tired, as you must be, so I shall retire. Cait will show you to your quarters when you are ready to sleep. Good night, Baron De-Lanyea. Good night, Sir Griffydd, Sir Trystan."

She looked at Dylan. "Good night, my lord."

"Good night for now, Genevieve," her husband replied.

Some time later, Genevieve sank onto the bed in her chamber and heaved a sigh of both relief and exhaustion as she pulled off her cap and scarf. She had managed to get a large chamber prepared for the baron and his sons, including furnishings and linens, all with only Cait's help, so that there was little disruption of the service in the hall. Although pleased with their efforts, she was now more tired than she had ever been in her life.

She was so tired, she didn't even feel like taking off her gown. Then she reasoned that perhaps she shouldn't. She wanted to make certain Dylan understood why she had been angry, and it would be better if she were fully clothed. Otherwise, he would probably kiss her, and caress her—and then she would forget everything but the delight of being in his loving arms.

Still, there could be no harm if she removed her shoes and put her aching feet up on the bed. She did so, shifting back so that she leaned against the substantial headboard.

Prepared for recriminations, Dylan found Genevieve sleeping thus when he arrived a short time later, after Cait had taken the baron, Griffydd and Trystan to a chamber in the west tower.

She looked so sweet and peaceful, all the creases in her brow erased, her bowlike mouth slack, her lashes fanning on her cheek, that all his rancor fled, to be replaced with tenderness.

Surely it was her teacher's fault that she was so particular and got so upset over every little thing. Give her time, he told himself, and she would soon find out that she could forgo some of the incredibly high and rather ludicrous expectations and standards she set for herself.

He pulled off his boots, then his tunic, flinching when he did so, for he had pulled a muscle trying to grab a recalcitrant sheep that had run the wrong way.

Better yet, he thought with a smile, she should have children, and then she would mellow.

Genevieve shifted beneath the coverlet and sighed as she awoke to the sound of hushed voices.

"Dylan?" she asked sleepily, sitting up and looking around in the still-dark room.

"Aye, it's me," her husband said from the vicinity of the door.

She peered at him in the gloom and realized he was talking to a woman, barely visible on the other side of the door. Cait, she thought. "What is it? Is something wrong?"

"No. I asked Cait to fetch me at first light, for I intend to return to Craig Fawr with the baron, to help with his gathering."

"You are going away?"

"Just for today, unless the weather turns bad. My uncle has a lot of sheep to get down from the hills."

"Has he not tenants enough for such work?"

Dylan said something softly to Cait before turning back and closing the door. He approached the bed. "We do it because it helps us get to know our tenants and the shepherds, and they get to know us. That is how loyalty is made.''

"I had not thought of that.''

"I don't enjoy tramping about the hills looking for sheep, you know. I would rather stay here with you.''

"I suppose you must go?''

"Aye. I would have said something of this last night, but you were already asleep when I got here.''

"Oh.'' Her brow wrinkled as she glanced down at herself. "I slept in my clothes?''

"You make that sound as if it was the same as committing murder,'' he observed. "I didn't want to wake you.''

Something was sticking into her hip. She shifted and pulled out her scarlet cap, now crushed. "I liked this cap,'' she said mournfully.

"I didn't see it,'' Dylan admitted, "or I would have moved it.''

"You might have wakened me so I could remove my dress,'' she said. "The wrinkles may never come out.''

"You looked so peaceful, I didn't have the heart.''

She glanced up at him, then away when she encountered his smiling face and sincere eyes. She remembered she had been angry with him for not mentioning the possibility of his uncle's visit; this morning, that didn't seem quite so important. "I must have been sleeping soundly."

He sat beside her on the bed. "We both must be sound sleepers. Let us hope an assassin never decides to sneak into our bedchamber. We wouldn't have a hope."

"Are you expecting an assassination attempt?"

"No! *Anwyl,* I have done my best to make sure I have no enemies." He regarded her mischievously. "I think the only enemy I might have is Lady Katherine DuMonde, for teaching you to be so particular."

"She trained us to be good chatelaines," Genevieve replied, again demonstrating that she was not above pouting. "I should think you would be pleased to have some order brought to Beaufort."

"Oh, I am—as long as it does not impede my pleasure."

"Dylan, you must know that the organization of—"

"Shh!" he said, putting his finger over her lips to silence her. "I know that things were in a mess, and you are straightening them out. I know my uncle and cousins probably had a better night's sleep in the west tower than they might have had in the hall. But I also know that doing things in what is supposedly the proper way is not important enough to me that we should be cross with each other over it."

"But—"

He looked like a contrite little boy. "But you would rather be cross with me?"

"No, of course not."

His smile was like the first sight of green grass after a long, cold winter. "Then we shall hear no more of Lady Katherine and the proper way. We do not stand much on ceremony and propriety here, and you will be happier if you remember that."

He leaned forward and kissed her lightly on the forehead. "Now I had better go, or my uncle will be out and on the road before I have had a bite to eat."

"When will you be back?"

"I will try to come tonight, for the moon should be full. If it rains or looks cloudy, though, I'll have to stay at Craig Fawr, although—" his lips turned up into his devilishly seductive smile "—I think it would be worth risking my neck to get back to you tonight."

She shook her head solemnly. "I do not. I have no wish to be a widow so young."

He laughed softly. "Well, then you may have to endure my absence tonight."

"I will try." A thought came to her mind, and she flushed guiltily, looking away.

"What is it?"

"It is an unworthy thought. I won't say it aloud. Indeed, I know I am wrong to think it...."

"What?" he demanded, his tone suddenly so commanding, she could not ignore his order.

"Am I the only woman who will have to endure your absence?"

He rose abruptly. "I am not married to anyone else, am I?"

She raised her eyes and spoke with very real and deep contrition. "Forgive me, Dylan. It was something Mair said, that's all. Well, that, and all those other women."

"What did Mair say?"

"She made no accusations," Genevieve hastened to reply. "It was just something about Cait. I'm sorry," she repeated.

"You should be." Then his expression softened. "Although, to be fair, if I were not married and Cait were willing, that might be a different story. But I am married, so now it doesn't matter a whit if Cait is willing or not, for I am not."

He grinned ruefully. "And there will be no

woman warming my bed at Craig Fawr or any-where else except here.''

His expression suddenly grew more serious. "I trust you will have no lover when I am gone?"

"Dylan DeLanyea!" she cried, aghast. "I would die before I would dishonor myself, or you!"

"This from a woman who crawled into my bed," he noted gravely.

She scrambled to her feet and glared at him. "That was different. I wanted to marry you."

"Then I can forgive your outrageous behavior, as you forgive my little errors," he said, dancing backward, his eyes twinkling merrily. "And you know, Genevieve, that I must absolutely trust you, or I wouldn't be able to tease you about taking a lover."

Her mouth fell open. "Oh."

"Oh, indeed," he said, his eyes darkening as he glided toward her with that animal grace only he possessed.

"When you look like that, I have to do this," he murmured as he pulled her into his arms for a passionate kiss.

It was so difficult to remain angry with him!

Nevertheless, she pulled away a little and chided him. "*Little* errors? I do not call neglecting to tell me that your relatives are coming a *little* error."

"They've slept in plenty of worse places than my hall, I can assure you. As long as they are warm and dry, that's all that matters."

She sighed softly as his lips brushed her cheek. "I know you care nothing for propriety, my lord, but I thought you wanted to have something to eat before you left with the baron."

He cursed softly as he gently pushed her away. "Propriety is one thing, punctuality is another— and the baron greatly esteems that quality. So, much as I would far rather linger here with you, my temptress, I had better be on my way."

He kissed her once more, swiftly, then hurried to the door. "I will try to return tonight, Genevieve, for now that I am an old married man, I find the prospect of sleeping in a barracks full of soldiers decidedly distasteful."

Unfortunately, the weather changed that afternoon. Clouds rolled in from the north, bringing with them not only a blast of frigid air, but drenching rain as well. The storm came up so suddenly that several of the men, Dylan among them, were caught out on the hills. They hurried to complete their task, but finally had to stop. The sheep were all running to the places of shelter that could be found on the hills, and not even the barking, running, nipping sheepdogs could persuade them to move anywhere else.

Even more unfortunately, when Dylan woke the next day, the weather showed no signs of any improvement.

Therefore, he went to his uncle's hall in no very good humor. The baron, Griffydd and several of his tenants and shepherds, with their dogs, were already gathered there by the time he arrived. The dogs eyed him, then went back to foraging beneath the tables. By the looks of things, he had missed breaking the fast and he would have to forage for scraps on the table like the dogs under them.

"It is a good thing I set men to gather the day we went to Beaufort," the baron observed as he grabbed the heel of a loaf from a nearby table and joined them. "The men got a good start without us."

"Still, it will not be good if this rain keeps up," Griffydd replied. "The lambs will be drowned minutes after they're born in wet like this."

"Seen worse, me," one of the old shepherds offered after a throat-clearing spit into the hearth. "A day or two at most, this, and then it'll clear."

"Since I have never known Elwyn to be wrong, I think we can all take heart," the baron declared. "Now, where is—ah, Dylan!" he cried, catching sight of his nephew. "Getting lazy now that you are a married man, is it?"

"Nobody came to fetch me," he replied, tossing the last bite of the bread to one of the dogs.

"And he is not used to sleeping alone, either," Griffydd said gravely. "All that space to himself must be confusing."

Dylan ignored that comment. "I think I am not the only one late rising. I do not see Trystan among you."

Dylan was surprised to note the baron's sudden frown.

"No, he is not," the older man replied.

"Taking after his fine cousin, perhaps, and with a woman somewhere, is he?" Dylan proposed, breaking the unexpected tension. "He is handsome enough, although I must say I think he lacks charm. Too like his older brother to really attract the women."

The tenants and shepherds chuckled and exchanged amused looks. This was an old jest of long standing between the two young men.

"Since it looks to rain the rest of today, at least," the baron said to the men in the hall, "I give you leave to return to your homes. You will be summoned when we can begin again."

The men nodded and began to leave, until only the baron, Dylan and Griffydd remained.

"So, where has Trystan got to?" Dylan asked.

"He's gone to visit Hu Morgan," the baron replied.

Morgan had been fostered in the baron's household years ago. A fine knight, he had married a Norman noblewoman and was now the father of three sons and two daughters.

"I am surprised you could spare him at this time of year."

"He wanted to go, and I saw no reason to withhold my permission."

That sounded reasonable enough, yet Dylan knew the baron too well to be completely sanguine about this explanation. The baron had let Trystan go at this busy time of the season—or sent him away—because he thought it best for Trystan to be gone.

Again, suspicion and jealousy entered Dylan's heart, and he struggled not to betray his feelings—not in front of the baron, who was like his father. Not before Griffydd, whose own high moral standard would take offense at the merest hint of dishonor in himself, or his family.

He would remember that Trystan had been raised by the most honorable man Dylan knew. If the young man's feelings were cause for concern, Dylan reminded himself, he could take comfort in the fact that Trystan was far away. By the time he returned, he would surely have tamed any wayward feelings for his cousin's wife, or found another young woman to pine for.

"So then, where can a man get a bite to eat?" Dylan asked jovially.

"Don't tell me you've forgotten the way to the kitchen," the baron demanded incredulously. "You, who used to distract my maidservants until we had to ban you from there?"

"The banishment is lifted, I hope."

"Since you are married, aye, it is."

"Good, because I am starving. Excuse me, my lords," he said, turning from them.

"You would do better not to be late for meals," Griffydd said.

Dylan waved his hand in airy dismissal as he strolled toward the kitchen.

Genevieve sighed as she stood in the door of the hall and stared at the driving rain. If this kept up, it was certain Dylan would not return tonight, and if it continued into the next day, she would not see him then, either.

Suddenly, and to her dismay, a tall, female figure, swathed in a cloak and carrying a bundle, appeared at the inner gates. She said a few brief words to the guards in a voice that confirmed Genevieve's suspicions.

Why was Angharad coming to the hall and why had the rain not kept *her* at home?

Genevieve was about to turn on her heel and flee to her bedchamber when she realized that Angharad had seen her. Worse, the woman had a smug, self-satisfied smile on her face as she came striding closer, as if she knew she had the upper hand.

Genevieve's pride asserted itself and she marched into the hall to wait for Angharad's arrival. A few servants were laying fresh rushes and she ordered them to stop. They could continue that later; in the meantime, they had other tasks she had set them, outside the hall.

Taking her position in front of the hearth, which sported a bright blaze that warmed the entire room. Genevieve straightened her shoulders and prepared for battle.

Which was not long in coming. In another few moments, Angharad was inside the hall. She threw back her hood and surveyed the room, then Genevieve, with an infuriating impertinence.

Her thick dark hair curled about her face, and

her dark eyes seemed full of life, a passionate match to her handsome features. It was not difficult to understand how a man would find her attractive, a realization that did not comfort Genevieve.

Despite that, Genevieve kept her tone level as she said, "Good day, Angharad."

"It would be a better day if it were not raining fit to drown a body, my lady," Angharad replied as she approached.

"I am surprised you would come here, then, in this rain."

"I wanted to bring this," she replied, holding out her bundle. "A wedding gift it is, for you and Dylan."

Genevieve supposed this woman had the right to refer to her husband without his proper title, but the lack rankled nonetheless. Still, she overlooked it as she stepped forward to accept the present.

It was woolen cloth, very finely spun and woven, and dyed a pretty, unusual shade of blue.

Genevieve couldn't help being rather sorry it was so excellent.

"He's gone for the gathering at Craig Fawr, is it?" Angharad asked.

"Yes."

Angharad's gaze grew even more intensely scrutinizing. "You are not with child yet."

"I..." Genevieve swallowed hard. "That is none of your concern."

Angharad came yet closer, her eyes seeming to bore into Genevieve.

"You are barren."

Chapter Twelve

Genevieve's hands tightened on the bundle she held over her cramping stomach.

Forever after, the scent of damp wool would remind her of this moment, and the horrible sense of inevitable prophecy Angharad's words engendered.

"You don't know that," Genevieve managed to reply.

"Don't I?"

"You *cannot* know that," Genevieve said, her voice slightly stronger as she came to believe it.

"I know it."

For the first time, Genevieve thought she saw pity lurking in the woman's eyes—and it was this pity that filled her with new dread. "How...how can you? Are you a witch?"

"No, not a witch. But I know things," Angharad

said evenly. "I knew I would bear Dylan a son, and that our son would grow into manhood. I know that Trefor will take his rightful place as lord of Beaufort. And I know that you will never bear a child."

"Get out!" Genevieve cried, clutching the wool so tightly a stream of water ran onto the stone floor. "Get out and never come to this hall again while I am mistress here!"

With a smile that was both sympathetic and triumphant, Angharad turned away.

Genevieve watched her leave the hall. Then she threw the bundle on the ground and ran to her bedchamber, slamming the door behind her.

Her hand went to her stomach.

"She cannot know!" she whispered fervently. "She is jealous and hateful, that's all."

Genevieve commanded herself to believe that, in spite of the look of genuine sorrow that had been in Angharad's eyes.

Three days later, Dylan finally returned. Exhausted, he saluted the sentries and slumped in the saddle while the gates opened to admit him.

As he had left Craig Fawr the moment they were finished the gathering, it was late in the afternoon by the time he rode through the puddled outer ward of Beaufort. The clouds threatened more rain, but he had been determined not to spend another night away from home.

Once in the courtyard, he slipped from his horse and strode toward the hall. It struck him that something seemed to be different, but he was more interested in getting some food and dry clothes and seeing his wife again—especially seeing his wife again—to figure out what it was.

Before he reached the entrance, however, the door flew open and Genevieve ran out.

"Dylan!" she cried, rushing into his arms and hugging him tightly.

He held her close, savoring her welcome. "Did you miss me?"

"Of course I did!" she replied, her breath warm on his chest where his tunic lay open.

"I didn't think I would be gone this long."

"If I had known you would be, I would have begged you to stay."

"Well, I am back now, and the baron has his sheep down," he replied, pulling away to smile at her.

His brow furrowed slightly when he saw how pale and tired she looked. He should have returned sooner, despite the rain.

"Has it been very difficult for you, with me

gone? Have the servants given you trouble?'' he asked as he took her hand and led her into the hall.

"The servants have been most obedient,'' she replied.

"Good.''

Inside the hall he felt the encompassing warmth coming from the blazing hearth. Before, when he had come home after a journey, even in the wet, there had not been a fire to welcome him.

He suddenly realized what had been different outside.

There hadn't been a pile of wood by the kitchen, and the well had a new roof.

"I have our chamber prepared for your return,'' Genevieve said, turning his thoughts in another, much more interesting direction, "and I told Cait to take some food there for your refreshment.''

"You must have missed me indeed, to want to have me so soon in the bedchamber.''

She flushed slightly, but did not smile.

Concerned, he nevertheless thought any more questions about what had gone on during his absence could wait until they were alone. He quickened his pace, noticing the fresh rushes and sweet-smelling herbs beneath his feet, and the lack of cobwebs, and that the tables gleamed from being polished with wax.

None of those things was nearly as important as being with Genevieve again.

In another few moments, and after passing a group of serving women who smiled and nodded but seemed surprisingly subdued, Dylan and Genevieve were in the bedchamber. A steaming bath awaited him, with fresh linens laid around the edge for padding. Another pile of thick linen lay nearby. On a small table was a carafe of wine, a loaf of bread, cheese and a basket of apples. A brazier provided welcome heat.

All that was lacking, he thought with a grin, was the bedcovers pulled back in anticipation.

Thinking of that, he turned to his wife, who frowned worriedly. "I hope the bathwater is not too cool."

"It looks fine to me," he answered, pulling off his wet cloak and nonchalantly beginning to remove his clothing.

"If you do not hurry, you may take a chill."

"I won't," he assured her. "I am feeling quite warm."

He glanced at her as he tugged off his damp breeches. "Have you taken a chill? You look pale."

"I am not sick."

"Glad I am to hear it. You look tired, too. Have you not been sleeping well?"

He stepped into the warm water with a grateful sigh, then sat down with another. He closed his eyes and leaned back against the edge. "This is perfect."

He opened one eye to regard her. "I confess I slept poorly, too."

"You did?"

He closed his eyes and slid deeper into the tub. "Aye. I missed you, Genevieve."

"I missed you, too. Very much," she whispered close by.

He heard a small splash and felt the water ripple. He opened his eyes as she leaned over the tub and, with her sleeve rolled up, proceeded to soap his chest.

This was so delightful, he didn't speak but simply enjoyed the sensation.

"If you move forward, I can wash your back," she murmured.

He obeyed and let out a low groan of pure enjoyment at her ministrations. "Perhaps it is worth leaving you for a little, if I am always to have such a reception when I return."

"I would rather you did not go," she said, and there was no answering teasing tone in her voice.

He grabbed her hand, turned and gazed into her face. She *was* pale, and tired—and suddenly an explanation for both jumped into his head.

"Genevieve, can you be with child already?" he asked happily.

"No. The day after you left, I..." She took a deep breath. "I am not with child."

"Oh."

He tried not to sound as disappointed as he felt as he faced forward again. "Well, not yet, anyway."

She resumed soaping his back. "No, not yet."

At the mournful sound of her voice, he again turned to regard her intently.

"Something happened when I was away," he said, and it was not a question. "Something to upset you. What?"

"We can talk about it when you're dry."

"Then I will get out now and get dry."

"You do not have—"

She fell silent when he rose and reached for a large square of dry linen. He quickly got out of the tub and briskly dried his body. She fetched him a dry tunic, breeches and stockings. When he was dressed, he said, "Now, tell me."

"You must be hungry," she replied, not meeting his gaze. "There is bread and—"

"I will not even sit down until you tell me," he said sternly.

Genevieve had counted every moment he was away, anxious for him to return so that she could speak to him of Angharad's words, and yet now, when the time had come, she felt even more frightened to speak of it.

"Well?"

"It is nothing. A woman's foolishness, that's all. I am not used to the Welsh, so surely…" Her voice trailed off feebly.

His severe expression softened and he came to her, taking her gently in his strong arms. She could hear the soft beating of his heart in her ear, a sound of comfort. "Tell me what—or who—has upset you, Genevieve."

She could not resist his gentle plea. "Angharad."

The beating of his heart quickened, and that sent new shivers of dread along her spine. "What did Angharad say?"

"She said…" A sob choked her.

He cupped her chin gently and raised her face. "What did Angharad say?" he repeated softly.

"She said I was barren," Genevieve whispered as a tear slipped down her cheek.

He seemed to go utterly still, and for an instant,

even his eyes looked blank. And then he tried to smile. "Pay no attention to Angharad."

His words gave her no comfort.

"Is she a witch?"

"No."

She took him by the shoulders and searched his face, seeking the truth—and finding it. "But you believe her."

He twisted away and ran a hand through his damp hair. "No, I do not."

"Do not lie to me, Dylan. You think she is right."

He went to the table and poured some wine into the goblet.

"You know she is right!"

He went to pick up the goblet, then hesitated, finally looking at her with anguish in his eyes. "No, I do not know. But I fear...."

"You think she might be right."

He nodded.

"Yet you say she is not a witch!"

"She practices no dark arts, or I would know of it."

"Then she is a seer?"

"Aye, or so she says."

He went to her and took her hands. "Genevieve, perhaps she is wrong."

"Has she been wrong before?"

He shrugged his shoulders. "She has dreams, and sometimes—"

"Sometimes?"

"Often," he amended, "they appear to come true."

"When has she been wrong before?"

"Genevieve, only God can truly know our destinies."

She looked at his strong hands holding so tight to hers. Her husband's hands. Her lover's hands. "I want so much to have your child, Dylan," she whispered.

He gathered her into his arms and tenderly stroked her hair. "Forget Angharad's words, my love, and believe that no mortal person can know what the future holds for any of us."

Then he kissed her, and as he did, he vowed that he would try to believe that, too.

"Now, what else has happened while I have been away?" he asked with a smile as he moved away toward the table. "Have any lambs come?"

"I don't know."

He gave her a quizzical look. "Didn't Thomas tell you?"

"He came this morning. He said he wanted to speak to me, but I told him if it had to do with the sheep or the farming, he should wait for you. I know nothing of such matters.''

Dylan took a few moments to select an apple. "I see.''

"I really don't know anything about sheep, Dylan.''

He tossed his apple into the air and deftly caught it before facing her, smiling. "I will have to send word to Lady Katherine that she has failed in teaching my wife.''

"I know a lot about wool, though.''

"Well, glad I am to learn you are not going to be completely useless to me.''

She flinched at his flippant words, and he was immediately contrite, throwing the apple back into the basket before he hurried toward her. "Forgive me, Genevieve! I spoke without thinking.''

"As long as you did not mean it," she said, trying very hard to smile.

"I assure you, my lady," he said in deeply seductive whisper, coming closer, "you are becoming very necessary to me.''

She went to him and wrapped her arms around him. "And you to me," she replied softly.

She rose on her toes and kissed him passionately, needing to feel his desire for her in a way she had not before Angharad had come to the hall.

"Let us make a child, Dylan," she whispered as she pressed more kisses to his stubbled chin, his neck, his chest.

"Right now?" he answered hoarsely. His hands gripped her waist as her lips continued their downward path. "What about your woman's—?"

She had forgotten that this might not be the best time.

She lifted her head to encounter his rueful countenance.

"Not that I would say no—"

"You are right."

"Nevertheless, I must learn to watch my tongue."

He brushed back a curl from her forehead, then lightly kissed the spot. "But we have plenty of time, Genevieve, and I will do my very best to give you a baby."

She nodded, believing him. Loving him. Needing him in a way she could never have conceived of even three short days ago.

"Now I had better go see Thomas and find out about my flock."

"And I had best see that preparations are under way for feeding the men when they return."

He held out his arm to escort her, and led her from the bedchamber. When they were going down the curving stairs, she said, "Dylan, there are some things I must ask you."

"Such as?"

"I found a bundle of unwashed wool in one of the storerooms. May we use it, or do you wish to sell it?"

He shrugged his shoulders. "Use it if you need it, sell it if you don't."

"But which would *you* prefer?"

"Sell it, I suppose."

"Some of the servants need new clothing. That wool could—"

"Then use it."

"The wine I wanted to buy is more expensive than I expected. If we buy five casks, the wine merchant will lower the price a little, but that is a large quantity, considering that most everyone here drinks ale instead."

"What do you think would be the better course?"

"That is for you to decide, since it is your money being spent."

He regarded her with a slightly furrowed brow. "Is this not household business?"

"Where the spending of money is concerned, I must have your approval."

"Then buy the five," he said.

"The fourth and fifth may sour before we can use it if we do."

Mindful that she had been upset earlier, he fought the urge to reply brusquely, all the while inwardly cursing Lady Katherine for instilling such deep-seated notions in her pupils. "Then tell the wine merchant I expect a good price, or we will buy none from him."

They entered the hall, where the servants were setting up the long tables.

"I already did. He came down two marks a cask from his original price. Now he says this is his last, best offer."

"If you think his price fair, pay it, and do so for any other purchases you need to make," he muttered, barely able to keep the frustration from his voice. "Now off I am to find Thomas."

Eight nights later, Genevieve sat in their bed and awaited Dylan's return. She had seen too little of him since he had gotten back from Craig Fawr, for it seemed the lambing had begun in earnest. He left at first light with Thomas and the other men, and returned late, to fall into bed too exhausted even to speak beyond a greeting.

But tonight, she thought, tonight would be dif-

ferent, for Llannulid had told her that the final two
ewes had lambed.

She surveyed the room. It was warmed with
coals glowing in the brazier, and three candles provided light. The shutter was slightly open to allow
the spring breeze to scent the air. The wooden tub
stood ready, half-full of warm water and covered
with towels to try to keep the water from cooling
too quickly. He had not used it the other nights,
but she thought he might tonight.

With slightly trembling fingers, she adjusted the
neck of her shift again before patting her hair,
which she had brushed with a hundred strokes.

And then her heart started to race, for she heard
Dylan's steps upon the stairs.

The door to the room opened and he came inside. Closing the door softly, he turned to face
her—and she gasped.

"Are you wounded?" she cried at the sight of
his bloody clothes as she scrambled from the bed
and rushed toward him.

"No, that's lambs' blood," he replied wearily,
holding out his hands to prevent her coming closer.

"We found an ewe whose lamb had died, and
another who had given birth to twins," he explained as he walked toward the tub. "Hill sheep
can forage plenty to provide milk for one lamb,

but not two. So we cut the skin off the dead lamb and made a little cloak for one of the twins, which we put close to the mother of the dead lamb. They smell the skin and thinks it's their baby, you see, so they allow the new lamb to suckle. In a few days, we take off the skin and the ewe accepts it as her own.''

He stripped off his soiled tunic.

As Genevieve went to uncover the tub, she tried to keep her teeth from chattering, for the stone floor was frigid on her bare feet. ''I hope the water is not too cold.''

''*Anwyl,* I stink—so it doesn't matter if it's as cold as that stream you pushed me in that day.''

''I didn't—you slipped.''

''Well, I don't remember much of that. It's you behind the bush sticks in my mind.''

''I recall that you flailed about like a demented bird.''

He smiled wryly as he put one hand on the rim of the tub to steady himself and tugged off his boots. ''Well, it was some day, anyway.''

He straightened, stretching. ''God's wounds, a lot of lambs is an excellent thing, but it's tiring when they come so fast together. We've got at least six black ones this year.''

''Oh?''

He glanced at her. "Your lips are turning blue, my love. Go, you, to the bed and warm yourself— unless you'd rather join me in the tub?"

She swallowed as he slowly, and quite immodestly, peeled off his breeches. "No, no, I will wait for you in bed."

"Whatever you prefer," he said with a chuckle.

He sucked in his breath as he stepped into the tub. "God's wounds, this is cold."

"Perhaps you should—"

She fell silent when he started to splash the water all over himself. And the linen. And the floor.

"Dylan?"

"What?" he answered, looking at her questioningly.

Forgetting about the slopped water, she started to laugh.

"What?"

"With that expression and your hair in your eyes, you look like a wet sheep."

"A wet sheep, is it?"

He climbed out of the tub and ran to the bed, jumping on it dripping-wet and naked.

"Dylan!" she cried, scrambling to sit up and get away from him. "You're soaking."

"Then help me get dry," he replied, burrowing under the covers.

"But you'll get everything wet."

His response was a muffled, "So what?"

"Dylan, what...what are you doing?"

His head popped out from beneath the covers, a devilish gleam in his eyes.

"I have not forgot what we are hoping to do tonight, Genevieve," he said, pulling her down beside him. "Come, wife, let's make a baby."

But they did not. Not that night, or the next, or any time through the whole of the following year, until Genevieve felt that if Angharad's words had not been prophetic, they had been a curse.

Chapter Thirteen

Genevieve stood at the window of her bedchamber and watched her husband in the courtyard below, laughing as he tried to teach Trefor and Arthur how to heft a broadsword. The children did not have real weapons, but ones made of wood that Dylan himself had fashioned during the winter. Silently she had watched him lovingly cut, carve and smooth them, while she sewed on a tapestry to cover one of the bare walls in the hall.

In the first months after her marriage, she had optimistically made baby clothes. By the end of summer, she had put the finished clothes and the fabric intended for more in the chest in the corner of the bedchamber, and they had lain there ever since.

"No, no, no," she heard Dylan admonish jovially. "Like this. Feet apart. Bent knees. Loose in the limbs, not stiff as an iron rod!"

He had been trying to get Arthur to stand thus for quite some time, yet he still possessed patience.

She surveyed the rest of the courtyard, and saw Cait standing near the well as she watched the lesson, an admiring smile on her pretty young face.

What was not to admire about Dylan, from his handsome face to his muscular legs, with the music in his laughter and the virility he seemed to exude with every breath?

He, too, realized he had an audience and called out something to Cait in Welsh, something Genevieve could not quite follow, for she still lacked anything approaching facility in her husband's native tongue. Whatever it was, though, it made Cait blush and giggle before she lifted her bucket and sauntered toward the kitchen, her hips swaying.

Genevieve turned away from the window, rubbing her temples and beginning to pace as she so often did these days. Her head didn't hurt; she was not unwell; yet more and more she found herself staying in her bedchamber, alone, walking back and forth as if doing so would make her feel better.

She had things to do, of course, that forced her to go to the hall and other parts of the castle. Orders to give and tasks to assign, with the result that the storerooms and chambers in the castle were a model of neatness with which even Lady Katherine herself could not have found fault.

At all times now, the servants did their jobs well and with dispatch, if without the levity that her husband's presence always seemed to engender among them.

Which was as it should be. Lady Katherine had emphasized again and again that the chatelaine of a castle must be respected if she wanted obedience and deference.

What Lady Katherine had not explained, Genevieve thought bitterly, was that it meant nobody seemed to like you.

Of course, respect and orderliness were important. And, Genevieve knew, if she could have a baby, she would be happy whether the servants liked her or not.

Occasionally, to break what was beginning to seem monotony, they had guests at Beaufort, the baron and his wife most often.

She had written to her mother's brother, the bishop, and as a result a new priest with impeccable education and a most appropriately holy manner had come to Beaufort. Of course, he was rather arrogant and aloof to the Welsh, but that was to be expected of a man who had been to Rome.

He didn't seem to mind being treated as an outsider.

Trystan remained at the castle of Sir Hu Morgan, although the baron expected to have his youngest son home later in the spring.

At least Angharad had not come to the castle again, and for that Genevieve was grateful.

She went to the door, flinging it open, determined to find something with which to occupy her mind, or at least see what Cait was up to.

She nearly walked right into Dylan.

"Ho, there, my lady!" he cried, grabbing her by the shoulders.

His gaze searched her face, as it always did these days.

"I should find out about the flour. Elidan can never seem to understand that I want the best, not the cheapest," she said, sounding peevish even to herself.

"That can wait," Dylan replied, leading her back into their bedchamber. "I have some news."

"Oh?"

He didn't look directly at her. "Llannulid is with child."

Not by Dylan.

That was the first thought to spring into her mind.

"How wonderful," she replied evenly.

Dylan had been half-afraid to tell her about Llannulid, yet that fear seemed groundless as Genevieve continued to speak without any appearance of dismay, except for the haunted look that lurked in her eyes these days.

"When is the baby due?"

"The autumn."

"Did Thomas tell you this?"

"No, it was little Gwethalyn. I met her with her mother in the village when I went to see what was keeping Arthur, and she told me she was going to have a baby sister. She can hardly wait."

He made a little smile. "She is so convinced it is a girl, I hope for her sake she's right."

"We wouldn't want anyone disappointed," Genevieve agreed.

Dylan frowned slightly at her tone, then he tried to dismiss it.

"Where was Arthur?"

"He spent the night with Trefor and Angharad. Mair had...company."

"Another lover?"

"I would think so."

"Who?"

Dylan shrugged. "I have no idea."

"Will she never marry?" Genevieve asked, and

this time there was no denying that she sounded annoyed.

"She claims she would rather have six pigs in the house than a husband," he replied, quite truthfully.

Nevertheless, Dylan almost wished he were with Mair, missing her honest frankness and spirited lovemaking.

He did not know precisely when it had happened, for it had been a gradual process, yet for some time now, his loving of Genevieve had become another duty she expected done, and done efficiently, as if it were only a task to be completed, or a chore to accomplish.

"I suppose we should be grateful she sends Arthur away when she decides to entertain a man."

"Genevieve!"

"I say only what any *decent* person would."

"She's not a whore."

His wife raised her eyebrows. "She only acts like one."

Dylan sighed wearily. He was in no humor to get into an argument today. They argued far too much as it was, about things both minor and major.

Indeed, Genevieve had grown so quick-tempered of late, he had taken to staying out of the hall to avoid her.

And although he was quite sure he knew the source of her constant irritability, he was getting profoundly tired of making excuses for her. "I think it's time we went on a journey."

"Where?"

"Craig Fawr."

"Why?"

"We have not been there since Christmas."

"I would rather not."

He crossed his arms over his chest. "We will have to go sometime, and we have left it late enough as it is."

When she didn't answer, he went to her, speaking softly, yet with firmness, too. "Griffydd's wife nearly died having the twins. Don't you think it's time we went to see her, aye, and the babies, too? You are always talking about duty and responsibility. It is our duty—and my wish—that we go, and I want to do so before the spring gathering."

Still she did not speak, and he put his arm around her. "Genevieve?"

She shrugged off his embrace. "Very well, my lord, we will go, as it is your wish and our duty."

"Good."

"When will we leave?"

"Tomorrow."

"Will you have servants accompany us? Cait, perhaps?"

"No, just us—unless you would prefer the company?"

"Not I."

He turned to go and glanced back at her expectantly, waiting for her to leave with him.

"I have one more thing to do here before I set the servants to preparing for the journey."

He nodded, taking some satisfaction from his success, then went to tell Thomas of his decision and offer his congratulations.

When he had gone on his way, Genevieve went to the chest in the corner. She reached into the bottom and pulled out two of the infants' garments she had made. They were little gowns, embroidered and carefully stitched, that would do for gifts for Griffydd's twin sons.

Three children in only two years of marriage...

She ran her hands over the soft fabric, then slowly she sank to her knees, clutching the tiny garments to her breasts that would never suckle a child.

And wept.

"So, Trystan is coming home, is he?" Dylan remarked to his elder cousin as they sat in the hall of Craig Fawr three days later. "It's about time."

"He had his reasons for staying so long with Hu, I'm sure," Griffydd replied, glancing at the far end of the hall, where his wife, Seona, sat near the warmth of the hearth.

Dylan followed his gaze, to see their eldest son on Seona's knee and the two cradles beside her. Lady Roanna was also there, cooing over the infants and, Dylan knew, keeping a maternally watchful eye on Seona lest she overtax her strength.

"Where is Genevieve?"

"Still dressing, I suppose."

"She was not in the hall to break the fast."

"No, these days she lingers at mass."

"Ah."

Dylan gave his cousin a look. "What do you mean by that?"

"Nothing, nothing at all," Griffydd replied, a look of genuine surprise flickering in his gray eyes.

Dylan leaned back in his chair.

"Forgive me, Griffydd," he said with a sigh. "I'm out of sorts today."

Griffydd fixed his shrewd and intense gaze on him. "Something is wrong with Genevieve. What is it?"

"Only the strain of being married to me, I sure."

His cousin ignored his attempt at levity. "Is she ill?"

"I don't think so."

"You don't sound very concerned."

"She takes her responsibilities very seriously, so she always looks tired and worried."

"I would say it is more than that."

"So now you are like Angharad?"

"I make no claim to be a seer."

"Good."

"Yet something is the matter with her—and you, too, I think."

"Oh, so now there is something wrong with both of us, says the man who tells me he is no seer."

"Dylan, she looks as if she hasn't had a decent night's sleep in weeks, and you scarcely much more. You haven't...?"

"Haven't what?" Dylan asked in a low, cold voice.

"She has no reason to doubt your fidelity?"

Dylan slowly rose. "If another man said that to me, I would kill him."

Griffydd also got to his feet, gazing steadfastly

at his cousin. "You cannot be surprised that one would have such a thought, given your past."

"What of her past? Perhaps she is unfaithful to me."

"Is she?"

"No."

"Then what is it?" Griffydd demanded.

Dylan scowled. "If I don't wish to discuss what should rightly be between only my wife and myself, I suppose you will be having your father take me aside for a paternal chat."

"You look like you need it."

"Maybe I should wait for him, then."

One of the babies started to wail, and both men paused to watch Seona hand her toddler to Lady Roanna and then pick up the hungry infant to put to her breast.

Griffydd turned back to regard Dylan with his unnerving stare. "She wants a baby desperately."

"I should think three would satisfy her."

"I was not meaning Seona, and you know it."

"Aye, I know it, and I know what Genevieve craves better than you."

"I want to help."

"And how would you do that? Perhaps you think you have so many children, you can spare one to give us, like giving a twin lamb to a ewe who's lost hers. Unfortunately, we are not sheep.''

"Dylan," Griffydd growled in a warning tone.

"I suppose I should have used rabbits for a better example."

Griffydd's hands balled into fists. "That is amusing, coming from you."

"Or maybe you think that you should take my place in Genevieve's bed?"

"Don't be a fool."

"Do you think you could do better? Or perhaps, after all your condemnations for my behavior in the past, you think it is fitting recompense that I have a barren wife?"

"Dylan!"

At the sound of his name gasped with pain and incredulity, he whirled around to see Genevieve standing nearby, her pale face growing paler.

"Genevieve, I—"

She ran past him, past Griffydd, past the women and the babies and out of the hall.

Dylan cursed softly and hurried after her. Unfortunately, the courtyard was crowded with servants, tenants, merchants and workmen on this fine day, and he could not see which way she had gone.

Nevertheless, he would find her and try to apologize for what he had said.

Although he more than half believed he had finally given voice to the truth.

Regardless of the chill in the air and the dampness, Genevieve sat on a fallen log near the bank of the river that ran past Craig Fawr. She had made her way through the village and into the wood knowing only that she wanted to be alone, and away from there.

Away from the women and babies.

Away from Griffydd's grave, gray eyes.

And most of all, away from Dylan.

She heard the sound of a horse nearby and rose quickly, wiping her tearstained face with the hem of her skirt. She was still close enough to the village that a scream would summon help, so she wasn't afraid of an attack.

"Genevieve?" the horseman called out. "Lady Genevieve?"

"Greetings, Sir Trystan."

The young man slipped from his saddle and threw his horse's reins over a nearby bush. "For a moment, I thought my eyes had deceived me."

"I didn't expect to meet you here, either."

She watched him approach. In the year since she had last seen him, he had changed somehow.

He was yet the same height and build; his hair

still brushed his shoulders, like that of all the DeLanyea men.

It was his face that had altered. It had lost the look of youth, somehow.

"What are you doing here, and alone?" he asked, running a scrutinizing gaze over her.

Unsure what the change in him meant, she said, "We came to visit your family."

Trystan halted a few feet from her. "I assumed that much. I meant what are you doing here in the wood all by yourself?"

She looked back to the castle where she could easily see the sentries on the wall walk. "There is no danger here."

A strange expression crossed his face as he took a long step closer. "Where is Dylan?"

"In the hall."

"Yet you are here alone, and unhappy."

She turned toward his waiting horse. "I am tired, that's all. Come, let us walk back together. Your family will surely be pleased to see you."

She went to go past him, but he reached out and gently put his hand on her arm, causing her to halt. "What has Dylan done to make you so sad?"

She lifted his hand from her arm and tried to regard him steadily. "Nothing. He has done nothing to make me downhearted or dissatisfied."

His gaze did not waver. "Someone has."

And then the expression in his eyes changed.

"Sir Trystan—"

"Trystan," he said softly.

"Sir Trystan, let us return to Craig Fawr."

"Will you not tell me what troubles you?"

He seemed so sympathetic, this young man, and kind. "It is Angharad."

"Ah," he said with a knowing sigh. "She told you something to upset you."

"I understand she has the Sight."

"Or so she wants everyone to believe."

"You do not think so."

"No."

"Why not?"

"Because the fate she claims to have seen for me is utterly ridiculous and absolutely impossible."

His skeptical words brought Genevieve more comfort than she had felt for many a day. "What fate is that?"

"She told me I would marry Mair—Mair!" he repeated scornfully.

For the first time in days, Genevieve smiled. "You make it sound as if Mair is the most ancient, ugly hag in Christendom."

"It would be better for everyone if she were.

She is an immoral, saucy wench who does not know her place."

"Harsh words, indeed!" Genevieve replied, all the while knowing she had thought the same thing.

Again that disquieting look passed over his face as he regarded her.

"I think I am being rather selfish, keeping you to myself like this. Come, let us go back."

He nodded. "Allow me to escort you, my lady. Will you take my horse?"

"It is not far. I shall walk."

"Very well."

She glanced at him uncertainly. Perhaps the emotion she thought she had seen in his eyes had been her own imagination—like the love she thought she had seen in Dylan's eyes a year ago.

This time, she truly hoped it was only in her imagination, for she had enough troubles without adding to them.

"Will you be returning to Sir Hu?" she asked as they walked toward the village.

The young man shook his head. "No. I have come home to stay."

"Your parents will be pleased."

"Yes."

"They have missed you."

"I had my reasons for being away."

By now, they had drawn near the village, close enough for a few villagers to notice them. They hailed Trystan, and she knew word of his coming would reach Craig Fawr before them.

"There will be a feast of fine things tonight, if I am not mistaken," she noted as they continued through the village.

"I daresay."

"Seona is much better."

"Good, is that. And my mother must be beside herself with pleasure doting on the babies."

"Yes, she is. But it is your father who seems the most delighted."

"I suppose that is because, at one time, he thought he would not be able to father children."

She gave him a surprised look. "He did?"

"You've seen how he limps?"

"Yes."

"There was another wound." The young man smiled at her. "Obviously, it healed."

"I wish such problems could always be so simply cured," she murmured wistfully as Trystan exchanged greetings with one of the smiths, whose teeth gleamed in his soot-blacked face.

Then Dylan appeared, striding toward them, on his face a look that held no welcome. Instinctively, her grip tightened on Trystan's arm.

"Genevieve," her husband began, "where the devil have—"

"Greetings, Dylan," Trystan said coldly, and as he did, he put his hand over Genevieve's, almost possessively.

She pulled away. "I went for a walk by the river, and—"

"And happened to meet him," Dylan finished. "What a delightful coincidence."

"Yes, it was, was it not?" she replied firmly, a slight frown puckering her brow. "You have not bid him welcome."

"Welcome, Trystan," he said brusquely. "We must hurry back, Genevieve. I have called out the guard to look for you. They will nearly be in the saddle."

He turned on his heel and marched back toward the castle.

With an apologetic glance at Trystan, Genevieve ran to catch up to her husband. Then she had to trot to match his long, swift strides.

"What is wrong with you, that you were so rude?" she demanded quietly. "What kind of greeting was that for your cousin?"

"If I am angry, blame yourself. How could you run off like that, without a word of where you intended to go?"

"I didn't know where I intended to go, except away from you!"

He gave her a scathing glance before returning to stare straight ahead at the looming castle gate. "So you simply happened to meet him, then?"

"What else?"

She halted abruptly and grabbed his arm, pulling him to a stop, regardless of who might be watching them. "What else?"

He shook off her hand. "I don't know," he growled as he began to walk again.

"Do not walk away from me, Dylan! I would know what you meant!"

He whirled around and gave her the most hostile glare she had ever seen him make. "For a woman who seems to regard her dignity so highly, you are apparently determined to make a spectacle of yourself."

Trystan came running toward them. "You should not speak to her that way!"

"Stay out of this, boy!"

"Of what would you accuse me?" Genevieve demanded.

"I am a knight, by God," Trystan declared, "and—"

"And Dylan is right. We should not air our grievances in public," Genevieve interrupted, suddenly aware that several of the villagers had come to hear the commotion.

"This *should* be a happy occasion," she finished. Then she marched past Dylan and into Craig Fawr, leaving the men to follow.

As they did, they scowled and glared at each other like two dogs forced to share a single bone.

Chapter Fourteen

By the time they reached the great hall, Dylan and Trystan had managed to conceal their true feelings beneath an appearance of congeniality, as had Genevieve. All three silently and simultaneously concurred that to display anything less than joy would ruin the pleasure of Trystan's return for the baron and his wife.

But that did not mean that Dylan was not anxious to get his wife alone. Unfortunately, he had to linger what seemed an age before Genevieve left the hall.

First, they had to wait through all the exclamations of surprise and delight at Trystan's return, then his revelations regarding Sir Hu and his family, who were all well and thriving and, indeed, to hear Trystan go on and on, the most wonderful family in the kingdom.

All through this endless talk, Genevieve sat and listened, scarcely bothering to so much as glance at her impatient husband.

The only thing that kept Dylan from demanding that she leave with him at once was the thought that she might have realized the seriousness of her error in departing from the castle earlier and was proudly putting off apologizing for as long as she could.

The moment they were alone, however, after she excused herself to change her gown before the evening meal, she disabused him of that notion.

She whirled around and glared at him the instant he closed the door. "Don't you *ever* do such a thing again!"

"What, wait patiently for you to decide it is time to leave the hall?"

"You know very well what I'm talking about," she retorted. "Don't you ever dare to speak to me in such a way as you did outside the gates."

"Tell me," he demanded just as hotly, "is it the words, or the place that upset you so? Is it merely that I spoke in public, and not the subject that concerns you, my high and mighty lady?"

"Your foolish, groundless suspicions are not worth discussing."

He strode toward her, halting so that his hostile

face was inches from hers. "That is something I
might expect a guilty person to say."

"Since we are speaking of infidelity, I shall have
to bow to your superior knowledge of how a guilty
party would act, my lord."

"I have never been unfaithful to you, Genevieve."

"No? Cait seems to find you fascinating."

"So what of that? So do a lot of women—that
doesn't mean I sleep with them."

"I suppose I should be grateful that you manage
to restrain yourself."

"Aye, you should."

"So, I am to be glad that you honor the vow
you made, and that you do not leave your wife for
another woman's bed, although apparently there
are hundreds who would welcome you."

She pointed imperiously at the door. "Go, then,
to another, if you would rather," she commanded.

His eyes narrowed. "Leaving you free to take
another man into yours? Or should I say, boy?"

"You are a disgusting, disgraceful, lecherous
villain to say that! My uncle was right! It has only
taken me this long to see it!"

"I am a man, and I know what I see."

"What is that? That I spoke for a little while

with your cousin, who was kind and treated me with respect?''

"Oh, yes, respect," Dylan snarled. "Whatever you do, you must have respect."

"Yes, I do and so do you—but at least I try to earn it. I do not neglect my duties because it is more important to be *liked*."

"It is good for you that you feel that way, since I can think of no one at Beaufort who likes you," he retorted.

Her face flushed. "I would rather have respect. I would not rely on charm and pleasing ways to lead my people."

"I will use what method I think best."

"Method? You would call lax leadership and jokes and charm a method? It is not. It is fear."

"What did you say?" he asked very, very softly, staring at her.

She faced him boldly. "You heard me well enough. You are afraid of them all, from Skinny Thomas and the commander of your guard to the lowliest kitchen boy or scullery maid."

"That is a lie."

"You are afraid they will think you are like your father and his father before him, and so you will do nearly anything to ensure that they think of you with affection—not respect, not loyalty, but affection."

"That's ludicrous."

"Is it?"

"Yes!"

He came toward her slowly, like a cat creeping up upon an oblivious bird. "No doubt young Trystan respects you."

"I hope he does."

"Has he declared his love for you yet?"

"He doesn't love me."

"No?"

The pink flush spread upon her cheeks. "He has said nothing to me about how he feels."

"He will. What will you tell him? That I lack respect for you? That you think I have been unfaithful to you? That you are sorry you married me?"

"*If* he does say any such thing, I will tell him I intend to honor the vow I made."

"Oh, so you are honorable and I am not?"

"I cannot say anymore what you are."

"*Anwyl,* I am your husband!"

"And I am your *barren wife.*"

Before he could respond, she spoke with a grim and terrible resolution. "Perhaps it is time we admit our mistake, Dylan. We married in haste, without knowing enough of each other. I will write again to my uncle the bishop. Surely he will be able to find some ecclesiastical reason to annul our marriage.''

It sounded as if she had been scheming to end their marriage for weeks. ''If that is what you want,'' he said slowly.

''I think it would be best.''

She was so calm, as if she were giving orders about a meal or some linen or a new gown, while he felt as if the floor beneath his feet had started to crumble away.

Now he knew all too well how Griffydd had felt when he thought his beloved wife was dying—as if he would rather die himself than live without her love.

But in the face of Genevieve's dispassion, reveal his anguished dismay he would not.

''Very well. Do what you must.''

''Under the circumstances, I will ask the baron if I may stay here until it is done. You can send me my things when you return to Beaufort.''

''If you wish.''

''I do.''

He nodded once, then turned on his heel and marched from the room.

Genevieve stood motionless for a long time, un-

Margaret Moore 265

til she heard someone calling Dylan's name in the courtyard below. She went to the window and saw her husband gallop out of the gate as Griffydd stood in the courtyard and shouted for him to stop.

She leaned against the window frame and told herself this had to be.

He deserved a legitimate heir and she could not give him one.

Seated in his solar with Rhys, his steward, Emryss DeLanyea looked up when he realized someone stood on the threshold. If he was surprised to see Genevieve there and with such a countenance, he kept it from his scarred face as he rose from behind the large table.

"So, there is plenty for a feast tonight, then," he said in a tone of finality Rhys recognized for the dismissal it was.

"Aye, my lord," the rotund steward said, getting up from the chair opposite the baron.

He turned to go and bowed to Genevieve. "My lady."

She acknowledged his greeting and entered the room as he left it. "I hope I am not disturbing you, my lord."

"No. Please, sit."

She did, in the chair recently vacated by the steward. "I hardly know where to begin."

"You could start by telling me where Dylan has gone, and in such haste."

"He went home to Beaufort."

"Is something wrong there?"

"No." She swallowed hard. "I have come to ask if I may stay with you awhile."

"Of course. But why?"

"I am going to write to my uncle the bishop, in London. I want him to find a way to end my marriage."

The baron stared at her. "Is it as bad as that between you?"

"Yes."

"Genevieve, since I allowed this marriage to take place, I feel somewhat responsible."

"There is no need."

"Will you tell me what happened? I have known Dylan all his life. Perhaps I can help."

"I do not think that is possible."

"Allow me to try."

He seemed so upset and so concerned, and she was so alone here, she decided there could be no harm in giving some excuse before rumor and gossip did it for her. "He is too lax."

"You know the why of that, I think."

"That doesn't make it right."

"It doesn't make it wrong, either."

The baron leaned forward. "Genevieve, I do not mean this to be a criticism, but I do not think you fully appreciate the legacy he has to struggle against. His father and grandfather were the most hated and despised overlords in Wales, and with good reason. Can you not try to understand that he wishes to be different from them?"

"But must he be so—?"

"Yes, he must, or he would not be Dylan."

Frowning and wondering if she had been wrong to think the baron could be impartial, she continued. "I do not wish to sound petty, but I have worked so hard to make a pleasant home for him, yet he has never given me one word of thanks."

"You are right. You sound petty—but before you march from here in high dudgeon—"

Having half risen from the chair, she sat back down.

"—let me say it is only natural to hope for some measure of gratitude. He can be a thoughtless fellow, yet I'm sure he does appreciate your efforts, if he has never given voice to that. A word from me, and he would see his error."

She clasped her hands together. Perhaps, when all was said and done, the only reason she could give him was the truth. "I have left the most important for last. I am not a fit wife for him."

Baron DeLanyea fell back against his chair with surprise. "Not fit for him? Who dares to say such a ludicrous thing?"

"I cannot give him a child."

"Ah!" The baron rubbed the scar beneath his eye patch. "You sound very sure of that."

"It has been a year."

"I'm sure my wife would agree that it sometimes takes longer."

"We have been…diligent."

"I can believe that."

"I have not had a wound, my lord, so there is nothing to be healed."

"If you know that much, you know I can sympathize with your dilemma."

He spoke so kindly, she regretted her previous words. "Yes, my lord, but there is more."

"More?"

"Angharad said I was barren."

He frowned gravely. "Ah. Angharad. You believe her?"

"So far, she has been proved right."

"What did Dylan say about it?"

"He said not to believe her, but I know he does." She studied the baron's face. "Do you?"

"It doesn't matter whether I believe it or not. What matters is that you both do. Did he just learn of Angharad's prediction today?"

"No. We have quarreled and argued many times of late, about many things. Today was but the end of a long road we have been traveling. And now we have come to the end."

"I see."

The baron rose, sensing that she had no wish to discuss these matters further. "I had best go tell my wife that you are going to stay."

Regarding her sympathetically, he said, "Only one piece of advice will I offer you, my lady. Wait a little before you write any letters. Dylan is a hot-tempered man, and you are a proud woman. Give yourselves some time before you act."

"As we did not do before we married?"

"Since you put it in those words, yes."

She nodded, thinking they had had time, and time had only enlarged the breach between them.

"May I stay here in your solar a little, my lord?" she asked. "Things are in such a bustle with your son's return, I would enjoy the quiet."

"Certainly, my dear. Stay as long as you like, since I am done my business for today."

He went to the door, then turned back once

more. "Do not think every marriage but yours goes smoothly, Genevieve. They all have their trials."

She watched him leave, then let her mind rove to the first time she had seen Dylan, here in the courtyard. How bold and handsome he had looked! How wonderful his smile. How flattering his interest.

How young and foolish and full of dreams she had been.

"My lady?"

She started and jumped to her feet as Trystan entered the solar.

"What are you doing here?" he asked.

"I was thinking," she answered honestly. "Now if you will pardon me—"

He closed the door.

"What are you doing?"

He turned toward her, a look of desperation on his face. "I must tell you."

"I think there is nothing you can tell me that I should like to hear," she said sternly, guessing his intent.

"I love you."

"I do not want to hear this."

"But you must!" he cried, throwing himself onto his knees in front of her. "You must know how I feel about you! I have loved you since the first time I saw you!''

"You should not. I am a married woman.''

"Married to a man who doesn't deserve you!''

"This is ridiculous, Trystan. I am leaving.'' She started to walk past him.

"No!''

He grabbed her around the legs, almost knocking her over.

"Trystan, stop this!'' she commanded.

He scrambled to his feet and held her arms, staring at her intently. "Genevieve, I went away loving you, and I stayed away, thinking time and distance would cure me of loving you. Nay, hoping it would.

"Yet the moment you appeared in the wood, I knew nothing would ever cure me of this sweet madness. I love you with all my heart!''

"I am Dylan's wife.''

"He is a lascivious rogue who dares to accuse you of infidelity.''

"And if he saw you here, he would have good cause to accuse me. Let me go.''

"I only want you to listen, to understand. I love you, and I heard what you intend. Write to your uncle. Annul the marriage—and let me marry you.

I will be a better husband than Dylan could ever be!"

"How do you know what I intend?"

He flushed and looked away.

"It is hardly honorable conduct becoming a knight to listen at doors."

"A desperate man does desperate things."

"Then if you listened at the door, you will know why I cannot be Dylan's wife."

"I don't care if you are barren."

"But I do!" she cried, all the tension of the past weeks breaking forth as she rebuked him. "If I will not stay with the man I love because I cannot give him children, do you think I would ever marry another?"

"You love him?" Trystan asked incredulously.

"Yes," she replied softly, only now, when Dylan was gone, realizing just how much. "I do."

"He must not love you, if he would leave you here."

"You may be right."

"He will have another in his bed in a week."

"I pray it may be so," she lied. "I want him to be happy."

"And I want you to be."

Trystan reached out and clasped her hands in his in unconscious imitation of a gesture Dylan had made so often, and that served only to remind Genevieve of the man who had gone. "Dylan could never make any woman happy for long."

She thought of the days they had shared when they were first married, before the shadow of her barrenness crept over them. Not make a woman happy for long? She would never have tired of him, of his laughter and vitality, of his humor and his tenderness. And his passion.

"Please, Genevieve, do not refuse what I offer! I love you!"

She gently pulled her hands free. "I do not love you."

"You may, in time," he pleaded.

"No, Trystan," she said firmly, feeling as if she were at least twenty years older than he. "I will never love you, or any other man but him."

Trystan's brow furrowed as his lips curled with scorn, for it seemed he understood at last the finality of her words. "He does not deserve your loyalty."

"Perhaps not, but he has my love. He will always have it."

"Then I have misjudged you," Trystan said bitterly. "You are no different from other women swayed by his looks and shallow charm."

At his harsh, embittered words, she realized this

was not a love-struck youth standing before her, flushed with a feeling he thought was eternal devotion. This was a man, with a man's heart, a man's desire, a man's love. And a man's anger.

"Trystan," she said softly and sincerely, "would you have me be untrue to my heart? Would you want me to encourage you when I am certain that I can never love you? Do you not see how cruel that would be, or vanity of the worst kind?

"I like you too much, I respect you too much, to do that to you. Someday, you will find another, more worthy woman you will love, and who will return that precious gift."

"Like Mair?" he replied disdainfully.

Genevieve reached out to take his hand, hoping to offer him some kind of comfort, but he jumped back as if her touch were poison to him now.

He strode from the room. She heard his mother call after him more than once, until the door to the hall slammed shut with a dull thud.

Genevieve rubbed her temples and cursed her uncle for ever bringing her to Craig Fawr.

Then she cursed herself, because she had become a blight to these good people.

Chapter Fifteen

A month later, an exhausted Dylan strode into the hall of Beaufort. His hands were bloody, his body sweaty and his boots thick with mud. Behind him came a dispirited group of soldiers and shepherds headed by a subdued Thomas. The men glanced at one another uneasily the few times they took their gaze from their irate lord.

"We go again tomorrow, until we've killed every fox we can find," Dylan growled.

He halted, his hands on his hips, and surveyed his unkempt hall.

The tables were as they had been when they had left that morning, and looked as if they had not even been wiped off since then. A loosened cobweb floated in the air before him, and despite his less than pristine state, he could smell the stink of the rank rushes beneath his feet.

"I beg your pardon, my lord?" Thomas said uncertainly behind him.

Dylan turned on his heel to face the men. "I said, we go again tomorrow, first light, until we've slaughtered every fox we can find."

"But the lambing—"

"It is for that reason we go!" Dylan snarled, the image of the mangled, headless bodies of the three newborn sheep fresh in his mind.

A fox had done the bloody deed, then left the dismembered corpses lying in the bracken like a conqueror's savage prize. "I will not have my flock destroyed by foxes."

"As you wish, my lord."

Dylan saw his steward's displeasure and heard the weary mutterings of the men, but didn't care.

"Cait!" he bellowed. "Where is my food?"

The young serving woman appeared, twisting her apron nervously.

He strode up to her, glaring. "Why isn't food on the table? Is it too much to ask to be fed after a full day in the hills?"

He gestured broadly. "And this place is a disgrace! Just because my wife is not here is no excuse! I am the lord here, and by God, I expect to be treated like it!"

He spun around and upended the closest table with a crash that made Cait and all the others jump.

"I am going to wash, and by the time I get back, these tables had better be wiped off and food set out, or you'll all rue the day you were born. And tomorrow, I want these rushes cleared out and replaced. Do you hear me, wench?"

His harsh appellation made Cait redden, but he didn't care about that, either. He was the lord and master here, and he would have his hall as it had been, in the days when Genevieve was here.

Bringing order and organization, and presiding over his table with her watchful and lovely eyes.

"Well, move!" he ordered when he realized Cait still stood watching him.

He marched toward the stairs and upward to his chamber.

This room was in an even worse state than the hall, he noted angrily. What the devil did the maid-servants do all day while he was off tending to his estate?

It didn't used to be this way, even before he married Genevieve.

Did it?

He peeled off his tunic and tossed it on the un-made bed, then went to the washstand. The basin had not been emptied of cold, dirty water. He picked up the pitcher and turned it upside down over the basin.

Empty.

He went to the door and threw it open. "Cait!"

Swift steps sounded on the stairs as he strode to the basin, rinsing off the worst of the blood in the frigid, filthy water. He heard the young woman's softly panting breaths at the door.

Whirling around, he glared at her. "There should be clean water here! And hot!"

"My lord, I'm...I'm sorry," she stammered, flushing and looking away. "I...you gave no orders about that before you left this morning."

He stalked toward her. "Must I give you orders for every thing? It is not as if I expected a tub of scented water, is it?"

With her eyelids lowered and her face flushed, she shook her head. Her breasts rose and fell with every frightened breath.

It had been a long month, a month in which he had lived like a monk.

He reached out and tugged Cait into his arms.

She put her hands on his chest to hold him away from her.

"My lord!" she cried as his arms tightened about her.

"You want this," he crooned, telling himself he

spoke the truth and it was only surprise in her eyes. "You want me."

When he bent down to kiss her, she twisted her head away, struggling in his arms, and there could be no doubt that if he took her now, it would be against her will.

Even then, he might have ignored that truth. He might have overcome her struggles and the look of fear in her eyes to take what he wanted.

Like his father and grandfather.

With a savage growl, he shoved the terrified Cait away. "Get out!" he muttered.

Sobbing, she ran from the room.

What had just happened here? What had been happening to him ever since Genevieve had stayed behind in Craig Fawr?

He had become an ogre, a leader whose men looked at him not with affection, or even respect, but fear and dismay.

God's wounds, he was becoming a monster, a bitter, angry creature thinking only of himself and his own desires. He splayed his hands on the washstand and hung his head. God help him, he was becoming his predecessors, because he had lost Genevieve.

And had become lost himself. Hopelessly, helplessly, viciously lost and alone, as he had never been before.

As he would forever be, unless he could win her back.

Maybe it was already too late. No doubt she had written to her uncle the bishop with the same efficiency with which she had managed his household. Perhaps the annulment was already in progress.

And her rejection of him complete.

What was he going to do? What could he do?

He strode to the window and looked out at the darkening sky. Storm clouds piled on the tops of the hills, and he could see flashes of lightning in the black mass.

Only a fool would venture out into weather like this, and at night. Only a man with no pride would humble himself before a woman and beg her forgiveness.

Or perhaps only a man desperate to regain the love he had so stupidly, selfishly thrown away.

Genevieve sat alone in the baron's solar and listened to the drips falling upon the windowsill. A terrible storm had come up in the night, with thunder and lightning and lashing rain. It had lasted through the morning, then stopped with unexpected swiftness, as it had blown itself out all of a sudden.

Now, sitting at the baron's table, with the parchment and ink before her, she tried to find the words for the letter she was about to compose.

For it had been a month, and the time had finally come to write to her ecclesiastical uncle.

She had heeded the baron's kind advice and taken advantage of his hospitality, yet she could not do so for much longer, in all good conscience, for it was obvious by this time that Dylan was not coming back for her.

Why would he? she reasoned. He knew she was right to call an end to their marriage.

Just as she was right to have spoken to Trystan as she had. Since that horrible day, the young man had avoided her whenever they happened to be in the same room, and she likewise avoided him. If his parents suspected anything amiss, they mercifully kept silent and continued to treat her with warmth and kindness. Still, she could not stay here forever; therefore, she decided, she would write to both her uncles, one to fetch her away and the other to destroy her legal bond with Dylan De-Lanyea.

She reached for the quill. Latin, or not? Latin had never been her strong suit, and Lady Katherine had considered that the only terms women really needed to know in that language were legal ones, especially having to do with property, inheritance and marriage settlements. Not, unfortunately, annulments.

Therefore, the vernacular it would have to be.

She dipped her quill into the little clay vessel holding ink.

A voice shouted from the wall walk, and then another took up a cry of alarm.

She rose swiftly and went to the window. Surely it could not be an attack.

She anxiously scanned the upper wall, trying to see where the soldiers had massed.

Then she realized the disruption was in the courtyard below, centered upon a cart full of barrels that must have just come through the gates, for the huge wooden structures still stood open.

Genevieve leaned out of the window, trying to get a better look. A crowd had gathered around the cart and the familiar-looking woman near it, who was gesturing wildly.

It was Mair! Perhaps she had been attacked and robbed on the road.

The crowd parted as the baron and Griffydd arrived. A few brief orders were issued, then Grif-

fydd and his father lifted something—no, someone—from the back of the vehicle.

"Dylan!" she gasped as if a fatal arrow had
pierced her heart when she saw his limp body.
"Oh, dear God, no!"

Grabbing up her skirts, she tore out of the solar
and raced to the hall, reaching it as they brought
her husband inside. The baron and his son were
surrounded by a small crowd of servants and workmen as they laid him on a bench.

Genevieve pushed past Mair, then stood staring
in horrified disbelief at Dylan's pale face, sodden
hair, muddy clothing.

And his left leg wrapped in crude and bloody
bandages.

"Is he dead?" she asked, her voice strained as
if her own throat refused to say the terrible words.
"Tell me he is not dead!"

Before anyone else answered, Dylan opened his
eyes, looking at her with both anguish and happiness.

"Genevieve!" he whispered. "Did you send
it?"

She knelt beside him and took his cold hand in
hers, scarcely believing the joyful evidence of her
own eyes and ears.

"The letter to your uncle—did you send it?" he

asked in a voice that was more a croak than his wonderful deep tones. "Has he replied?"

"No! No!" she whispered, choking with relief, unmindful of the people around them. "I have not. I...I could not."

"Thank God! Thank God I am not too late. Don't," he said, a shadow of his former smile on his face. "I beg you to take me back."

The baron cleared his throat loudly, but Genevieve ignored him.

"Oh, my love!" she cried as she pressed his hand to her cheek. "You? I am the one—"

"Yes, you are the one wife for me, Genevieve, and I will have no other. I was a stupid, stubborn fool not to come sooner. Promise me you will not write to that uncle of yours."

"But—"

His grip tightened as he looked deep into her eyes. "It is you I want, Genevieve, more than any unknown, unborn offspring. You will be more than enough to make me happy. Please believe that and come home. I cannot live without you."

She did believe him, and her heart sang with joy at his fervent, sincere words.

"Yes, my lord," she replied, happiness in every word. "As I respect and honor you and—" her voice dropped to a soft whisper "—have been utterly miserable without you, I will gladly come."

"Thank God!"

For a moment, all they did was smile at each other.

Until, with a grimace, Dylan raised himself on his elbows and looked about him, his wry gaze coming to rest on Mair. "And thank God I'm not dead, nor dying, either, though I should be after the rough treatment I've had. Mair nearly broke my other leg getting me into that cart."

Mair's answer was an inelegant snort.

Dylan slumped back down, and Genevieve gently caressed his damp brow. "What happened? Were you attacked?"

"I wish it was something as grand as that, but I only fell off my horse."

"Because like a *gwirionyn* he insisted upon riding out last night, even though the storm was breaking," Mair declared, apparently annoyed, and yet there was admiration in her tones, too. "Should have left him on the road, me, if he's going to insult me."

"A charming sentiment, Mair," Dylan said as he made another grimace, although whether from the pain of his leg or at her speech, Genevieve didn't know.

Then he grinned. "You know you have my thanks."

"You found him?" Genevieve asked.

"Aye, I did, and it's a good thing I did." Mair's expression altered slightly. "Must have had quite a reason for doing such a stupid thing, I'm thinking."

"I did. Love."

"Let me through."

Lady Roanna hurried toward them and everyone parted to let her near. With deft fingers she began to undo the bandage. As she did so, Dylan's hands squeezed Genevieve's, and he cursed softly.

"It's broken," her ladyship observed briskly.

"I thought as much," Dylan muttered sardonically.

"I am going to have to set it right away. Everyone should leave except Emryss and Griffydd. Genevieve, please go to the kitchen and fetch some hot water, and tell Bronwyn I will need lots of bandages. And someone should prepare the chamber in the west tower."

"I'm not leaving," Genevieve said firmly as the servants and workmen began to depart. "Mair can go to the kitchen."

"This is not going to pleasant," Dylan said grimly. "I don't think you should be here—"

"*I* do." She regarded him steadily. "It is my duty."

His brow furrowed in a way that had nothing to do with the pain in his leg.

"And my wish," she added tenderly, and her reward was his smile.

Lady Roanna glanced at her husband and son, then nodded. "Very well. Emryss, you hold down one shoulder, Griffydd the other."

Her gaze softened with sympathy as she regarded Genevieve. "Don't look, dear."

Genevieve did look, and later, when she considered how Dylan had managed to keep mostly silent as Lady Roanna set his leg, she admired him all the more.

Now, she sat on a stool beside the bed upon which he lay, his face pale as he slept. Lady Roanna had insisted rest was the best thing, and prepared a draft to lessen the pain and enable him to sleep. While Genevieve wanted nothing more than to talk to him, she had deferred to the older woman's medical opinion.

Besides, she rationalized as she held his hand, she could just sit and look at him for hours anyway.

"My lady?"

She turned to see Mair in the doorway, a cup in her hand. "I've brought you something to drink, since you won't leave him."

Genevieve smiled. "No, I won't leave him ever again, unless he asks me."

Mair came into the room and regarded the slumbering Dylan with a sympathetic, even maternal expression. "He looks like an angel when he's asleep, though he's a devil when he's awake."

"I think he's an angel all the time."

"*O'r anwyl*, my lady, you must be deep in love if you think Dylan DeLanyea isn't Satan's own temptation in the flesh when he's awake and walking around."

Genevieve didn't answer as Mair handed her the cup filled with fresh, cold water.

"Lady Roanna thinks he might have a limp, he was so long wounded before I found him."

"As long as it does not get infected," Genevieve said anxiously.

"Oh, I wouldn't worry yourself about that," Mair replied. "Lady Roanna learned from old Mamaeth herself, that died this past winter. There wasn't nothing that woman didn't know about healing."

"Do you really think so?"

Mair smiled kindly. "Aye, my lady, I really

do.'' Then she got a mischievous twinkle in her eye. "Your holding his hand all night will probably help, too."

Genevieve looked away as an idea bloomed in her mind.

"What is it?"

"Oh, nothing important."

"Yes, it is," Mair declared, coming around the bed to stare at Genevieve in the most disconcerting way.

"I was just wondering if Lady Roanna might know if there is something I could do...some medicine I could take to get with child."

Mair frowned. "Ask her, if you like. But I would say a man who risks his life is deep in love, too, whether there will be children or not."

Genevieve started as Dylan's hand suddenly squeezed hers. She looked at him, but he still slept peacefully. Perhaps it was no more than a dream.

"I...I have been wanting to ask you this for a long time, Mair, because I think you are a sensible woman. Do you believe what Angharad says about the future?"

"I try not to listen to her at any time."

Genevieve continued to regard Mair steadily. "But do you believe her?"

"She has an uncanny knack of being right, I'm sorry to say."

"Oh," Genevieve said with a sigh. "Even about you and Trystan?"

Surprisingly, Mair suddenly looked angry and suspicious. "What about me and Trystan?"

"Don't you know?"

"No! And I don't want to know! Me and that prim, arrogant little squint? That's the stupidest thing I've heard in my life! I'd rather go without a man the rest of my life than be with that one!"

"Then let us all pray Angharad is wrong," Dylan said softly, opening his eyes to look from one to the other.

"You're supposed to be asleep!" Genevieve cried.

"How can a man sleep with all this chatter?" he demanded.

Genevieve flushed guiltily while Mair sniffed disdainfully. "How long have you been listening?"

"Long enough. Now if you will please excuse us, Mair, I have to have my rest. It felt like Lady Roanna was trying to twist off my leg when she set it."

"All right, then," Mair said sourly. She went to the door. "Glad I am you're not dead," she muttered as she went out and closed the door behind her.

"She doesn't sound very glad," Dylan observed wryly as he stifled a yawn. "*Anwyl,* what was in that potion?" He shifted and grimaced, although he tried to make it look like a grin.

"I misspoke, but I thought she would already know what Angharad said about her and Trystan."

"Nobody dared tell her. She's hated Trystan for years, and he doesn't like her, either. Now come here and sit by me. I will have you close as I can get you."

"If I sit on the bed, I might hurt your leg."

"Damn my leg." He grinned drowsily. "It's my arms you should be worried about, because I'm going to put them around you and never let you go."

"How can I refuse?"

Moving carefully, she gingerly sat on the edge of the bed. "Lady Roanna thinks you will have to stay in bed for a while."

"I will have to find a way to endure," he said with a mockery of resignation he took no pains to make sincere. "But I am anxious to get home, although you may not be when you see how things have fared without you."

"As long as you obey Lady Roanna's orders. I will not have you worse."

"Mair spoke the truth about Lady Roanna. She is very skilled in healing."

"I am glad to hear it."

Dylan moved slightly, turning his head to regard her tenderly. "You can ask her about the other, too. But believe me, Genevieve, it is you I love and need."

"I want to have your children so much, Dylan!"

"And maybe you will. Or maybe you won't. Either way, I shall love you just the same."

"Truly?"

"Indeed, I love you enough to go out into another storm as soon as one offers to prove it, broken leg or no."

"Promise me you won't do that!"

"You might change your mind, if I neglect to tell you how pleasant you made Beaufort. I'm sorry I never said so before. Can you forgive me for that, too?"

"Yes, if you can forgive me for being so fussy and particular, and cross all the time."

He caressed her satiny cheek. "You were worried and upset, and I should have done more to comfort you, and to make you see that your love is more than enough to content me.

"Genevieve," he continued gravely, "in a way, I shall be glad if you do not bear children. When I think of how Griffydd almost lost Seona—"

A woman's delicate cough made them turn toward the door, where Lady Roanna stood holding fresh bandages and the bottle of sleeping potion. "Mair told me you were awake, Dylan, and I came to change your bandage."

"I will do it," Genevieve offered, "if you will show me."

Smiling her calm, beatific smile, Lady Roanna came toward the bed. "Of course. I would be happy to."

The lesson proceeded apace, with only a few growls from the patient as they unwrapped and rebandaged his leg.

"The color is good, and he has no fever. You are a strong and healthy man, Dylan, and for that you should be thankful."

"I do have much to be thankful for," the pale, weary nobleman replied.

"So do we all," Lady Roanna agreed.

"You are very skilled," Genevieve observed.

"I had an excellent teacher." Lady Roanna glanced at her, and Genevieve was a little taken aback by the gleam of mischief in her eyes. "Although she was often cross and rarely patient."

Her regard returned to Dylan. "Drink this, and sleep."

"I don't want to sleep. I want to be with Genevieve," he said with a boyish sulk.

"Not even a broken leg will deter you, is that it?" Lady Roanna chided.

Genevieve colored, and Dylan grinned. "I didn't mean that—for once."

"Drink this," the lady ordered, and in a tone that clearly said the joking was over.

Dylan grudgingly obeyed, then lay back upon the pillow. "*Anwyl,* that tastes terrible. If I didn't know you better, my lady, I'd swear you were trying to poison me."

His eyelids started to droop. "Genevieve, as you love me and if I must drink it again, try and persuade her to make it taste better."

"I will, my love."

"Good. I know I can count on you...." His voice trailed off into a low sigh, and his eyes closed. In another moment, his chest rose and fell with the soft, even breathing of a slumbering man.

Lady Roanna looked at Genevieve. "He will sleep soundly for some time. Why don't you come to the hall and sup with us?"

"If you please, my lady," Genevieve said, "I would like to stay with him."

Lady Roanna smiled. "Since I have given him a sleeping draft strong enough for a horse, I suppose he—and you—will not get into any mischief, although," she mused as she looked at her foster son, "who can say what Dylan is capable of when he is so much in love?"

Genevieve blushed, and then resolved to ask her question. "Lady Roanna, Mair thought I should ask you.... I am not yet with child, and she thought...that is, I hope..."

Lady Roanna's expression grew tenderly sympathetic. "All I know is superstition, not medicine, for such things. When all is said and done, my dear, I think it is best to pray."

Genevieve smiled peacefully.

"I will pray and hope, my lady," the young woman replied softly. Then she looked at her sleeping husband. "But if I am not blessed with a child, I will take comfort in knowing I am still more to be envied than pitied, because Dylan DeLanyea loves me."

Lady Roanna hugged her tenderly. "You are indeed a lucky woman, Genevieve, and he is a lucky man. I am fortunate to know you both."

She drew back and smiled warmly. "I leave him to your care, then. Good night, Genevieve."

"Good night, my lady."

When Lady Roanna was gone, Genevieve carefully crept onto the bed to lie beside her sleeping husband. She put her arm over him lovingly, took his hand in hers and laid her cheek on his broad shoulder, happy and content.

His hand clutched hers tightly, for even though he slept, Dylan sensed that he was no longer alone. Genevieve was beside him, loving him as he loved her.

And he smiled.

* * * * *